ANDREA CAMILLERI

THE COOK OF THE *HALCYON*

Translated by Stephen Sartarelli

MANTLE

First published 2021 by Penguin Books,
an imprint of Penguin Random House LLC

First published in the UK 2021 by Mantle
an imprint of Pan Macmillan
The Smithson, 6 Briset Street, London EC1M 5NR
EU representative: Macmillan Publishers Ireland Limited,
Mallard Lodge, Lansdowne Village, Dublin 4
Associated companies throughout the world
www.panmacmillan.com

ISBN 978-1-5290-5335-7

Originally published in Italian as *Il cuoco dell'Alcyon*

1 3 5 7 9 8 6 4 2

A CIP catalogue record for this book is available from the British Library.

Typeset by Palimpsest Book Production Ltd, Falkirk, Stirlingshire
Printed and bound by CPI Group (UK) Ltd, Croydon, CR0 4YY

THE COOK OF THE *HALCYON*

ONE

He was dancing a waltz at the edge of a swimming pool, all pomaded and fragrant, and he knew that the woman in his arms was Livia, who just a few hours earlier had become his wife. But he couldn't see her face through the dense white veil that covered it.

Suddenly a strong gust of wind blew in, moving the veil just enough for him to discover that it wasn't Livia he was dancing with, but Mrs Costantino, his third-grade schoolteacher, replete with moustache and crooked glasses. The fright drained him of strength; he felt faint and shut his eyes.

When he opened them again, he found himself lying in the bottom of a small rowing boat dancing dangerously over hair-raising breakers as tall as houses. He realized at once that the boat was on its side and might therefore capsize in a moment. He had to do something, anything, without wasting another second.

He was still all dressed up, sporting even a fancy tie, but his clothes were so sodden with rain that they'd become practically waterproof.

The clouds were so low and black that they looked like a sort of shroud about to cover everything at any moment. A sign that the storm hadn't yet vented all its rage.

He hadn't the slightest idea how or why he'd ended up in such a situation. He vaguely recalled getting dressed up for his wedding, but that was all.

Suddenly he noticed that one of the oars was slipping out of the rowlock. He had to prevent this at all costs; if he lost the oar he would never be able to manage the boat.

He tried to stand up, but his clothes, sopping wet as they were, impeded his movements and kept him glued to the bottom of the boat.

He tried again, grabbing the sides of the boat with both hands, and managed to rise to a sitting position. Reaching out with one arm, he was able to touch the oar with the tips of his fingers, but then it slipped away and fell into the water.

How on earth was he going to get out of this now?

He absolutely had to get that oar back.

In one painful bound, he leapt to his feet, but immediately the wind struck him just like a punch, forcing him to his knees, blowing so fiercely that he couldn't keep his eyes open.

He kept them shut because they were burning so badly, but when he opened them again, in a flash he saw the bows of a gigantic sailing ship, heading straight for him. It looked like it was flying.

How could it not have been there just a minute before? Where had it come from?

Terrified, he decided at once that his only hope was to jump into the sea and swim as far away as he could.

And so he dived in, but the violence of the breakers, and the weight of his clothes, prevented him from swimming.

Desperate, he managed to go a few metres in the water.

Then he heard the crack of the wooden boat being cleft in two by the bows of the ship.

Maybe things would be all right now.

All at once, however, the waves began to grow in ferocity, reinforced by those created by the ship's propeller.

A first wave dragged him under, but he managed, he didn't know how, to come back up to the surface. He didn't have time, however, to catch his breath before a second wave nearly tore his head off.

He passed out and started sinking, sinking . . .

When he awoke he was sitting up in bed, out of breath, heart beating wildly, mouth agape, gasping for air.

Against the windowpanes, exposed by the open shutters, raindrops as big as chickpeas were drumming loudly. There was no light outside. It was unclear whether it was day or night.

He looked at the clock. Half-past six. Time to get up, in theory.

But what was the use of going out at that hour if all that awaited him at the office were stacks of papers to be signed?

His mood darkened. He got up, opened the windows, pulled the shutters shut, closed the windows, went and lay back down in bed, and closed his eyes.

*

'Isspector! Iss pass nine o'clock! Ya wan' me to bring ya somma coffee?'

Adelina's voice blared like the trumpet on Judgement Day, the one that wakes the dead.

He sat up in bed again. Past nine o'clock?

True, there was nothing he had to do, but all the same, it was bad form to show up at the office late in the morning.

'Sure! And make it snappy!'

The rain had stopped, but he could tell that the storm was merely taking a break.

His housekeeper came in with a steaming cup. He savoured the coffee down to the last drop.

'There's no watta, ya know,' Adelina informed him.

Montalbano took this hard.

'What do you mean, there's no water?! How can that be? With the deluge we've been having the past few days!'

'Whattya wan' me to say, Isspecter? There jest in't any.'

'So how am I supposed to wash myself?'

'I collicted a li'l bit o' water an' put it inna sink anna bidé. Y'er going to hafta mekkit be enough.'

'Where'd you collect it?'

'Sints I awreddy been 'ere f'r o'er an hour an' it wazza still rainin', I fill uppa tree pans an' a bucket witta watta fro' the gutta. Iss watta fro' heaven, an' so iss clean.'

Clean, my arse.

If it was from the gutters on the roof, chock-full as they were with the shit of rats, seagulls, and pigeons . . .

'You know what I say? I'm going to wash at the police station. And I'll get dressed there, too.'

He left the house in a bad mood.

He'd managed to escape, but just outside the door he found a lake and got his shoes all muddy taking the four steps he needed to reach his car.

He hated it when he got mud on his shoes.

He could have gone back inside and found another, clean pair of shoes. But was it right to show up at the police station with a pair of shoes in one hand and a little bag with clean underwear in the other? He turned the key in the ignition, but the engine didn't start. He tried again. Nothing. The car seemed dead.

No point in getting out, raising the bonnet, and looking inside. After all, he didn't know a damn thing about cars. He let off steam for five minutes straight, unleashing a stream of curses, head resting on the steering wheel. Then he got out and went back into the house.

'D'ja fuhget som'n?'

'No, it's the car . . .'

He was about to phone the station to ask someone to come and pick him up, when Adelina said: 'The watta jess cumma back, ya know.'

Water! This brought to mind a poem he learned in French class in junior high school:

Eau si claire et si pure,
bienfaisante pour tous . . .

He dashed into the bathroom. They were likely to shut the water off again at a moment's notice. There was no time to waste. Whatever the case, better to turn up late at the office than to arrive looking like some kind of refugee.

And now they even wanted to privatize water! The bastards!

But you could be sure there would still be shortages, no doubt about that, and they would make you pay a euro a drop.

Now all clean and shaved, he left the house again, made his way around the lake, and managed not to muddy his change of shoes.

Not until he stuck the key in the ignition did he remember that the car wouldn't start.

Except that this time it did.

It is said that man, in a democracy, is free. Really?

But what if the car won't start, the phone doesn't work, the power is out, there's no water or gas, and the computer, television, and fridge refuse to function?

It is probably better still to say that, yes, man is free, but it is a conditional freedom, dependent upon the whims of objects he can no longer live without.

And almost as if to prove him right, the car stopped running the moment he entered Vigàta.

Apparently it wanted to mess with his head.

He walked the rest of the way to the station.

*

'Cat, get me Fazio,' the inspector said as he was passing the switchboard operator's cupboard.

''E ain't onna premisses, Chief.'

'Then get me Inspector Augello.'

''E ain't onna premisses, neither.'

Had they all flown the coop? What was going on?

Montalbano took two steps back. 'So where are they?'

''Ey was called by Mr Drincananato, oo'd a happen a be—'

'I know who he is. What did he want them for?'

''E wannit 'em 'cuzza woikers was raisin' hell ousside the 'stablishment.'

Montalbano made a snap decision. 'I'm going to go there myself.'

He was about to set off when he remembered he didn't have a car.

'Is Gallo around?'

''E's onna premisses, Chief.'

'Then call him and tell him I need him to drive me there.'

'Bu', Chief, I guess I din't make myself clear. Gallo in't onn 'ese 'ere premisses, but on th' other premisses, atta Drincananato woiks, wit' Isspector Augello.'

'Is there a squad car available?'

'Yeah, we got one, Chief, 's far as 'at goes, bu' iss not in any condition to go nowheres, insomuch as iss got no petrol. Bu' ya c'n take mine, if ya want, I'll give yiz the keys.'

As the inspector was starting the car, it occurred to him that he should post a circular around town, saying:

GIVEN THE CUTS IN GOVERNMENT FUNDING, EVERY CITIZEN DESIRING THE PROTECTION OF LAW ENFORCEMENT IS REQUESTED TO COME TO THE POLICE STATION WITH TWO CANS OF PETROL.

WHOEVER DOES NOT CONTRIBUTE WILL NOT BE PROTECTED.

Trincanato, Inc., was a small factory specialized in making ships' hulls, and things had gone well there until two years ago. The company employed about two hundred people, office and machine workers.

Then the old proprietor died, and the business was passed on to his son, Giovanni, who only had eyes for women and gambling.

Between Giovanni and the sudden economic crisis, it wasn't long before the factory was in trouble.

Just three days earlier, in fact, Montalbano had learned that the layoffs were starting, and unemployment compensation claims were being filed.

Though he didn't feel like it, he was going to the site because he was afraid to leave Fazio and Augello alone there. Mimì was liable to say the wrong thing to the enraged workers, and that must be avoided.

He'd once had his head busted by angry strikers, but Mimì wasn't the type to learn his lessons gracefully.

There were about fifty people gathered round the gate of the large shed, which stood practically at the water's edge.

On the other hand, there was nobody outside the administrative building, which was protected by four private security guards with pistols in their holsters.

Everything was calm. Nobody was shouting. On the contrary.

The workers as well as the clerks all seemed strangely uncomfortable, and were either clustered in small groups of two or three or standing alone, heads bowed and looking at the ground. They weren't talking to one another.

Montalbano parked the car, got out, and headed towards Fazio, who had an arm around a man's shoulder.

As he drew near, he noticed that the man was crying.

Fazio, seeing the inspector, came up to him.

'So where's all the commotion Mr Trincanato was talking about?' asked Montalbano. 'It looks more like a funeral to me!'

'Indeed,' said Fazio.

'Speak more clearly,' replied Montalbano, feeling confused.

'Early this morning, a worker by the name of Carmine Spagnolo made his way inside the shed and hanged himself. He was fifty years old, and had a wife who's ill and three kids. He'd just been laid off.'

'But are things really so bad here?'

'The workers were ready to make some sacrifices, even to take a pay cut by half, but Trincanato preferred just letting the whole thing go to shit.'

'But doesn't he also lose out that way?'

'The workers say no; they say he gains from it. They say he made a deal with the competition.'

'Have you called the prosecutor and Dr Pasquano?'

'Yes, but the prosecutor can't come before one o'clock.'

'I want to see the body. Who's inside?'

'Gallo.'

Fazio then turned to the two guards standing stiffly outside the gate and said: 'Let us in.'

The dead man was hanging just three steps inside the entrance.

All Carmine Spagnolo had had to do was to climb up a half-finished hull, run a rope through a pulley, tie it around his neck, and jump.

He must have been a rather short, delicate man in life. If one ignored his bulging, desperate eyes and his mouth agape in a silent scream, he looked a little like a rag doll.

Gallo, despite a giant no-smoking sign, was standing there with a lit cigarette and a good ten butts on the floor at his feet.

'Chief, I'm just so upset. I can't stand looking at the poor bastard.'

'Then go outside. What are you doing in here, anyway?'

'No, sir, I'm going to stay here.'

'Why?'

'Since his mates aren't allowed to come in, I don't want to leave him all alone.'

Montalbano had to refrain from hugging him. 'Where's Augello?'

'In Trincanato's office.'

He went out. The sky was covered with black clouds again, and a cold wind was blowing.

'I'm going to talk to Trincanato,' he said to Fazio, heading off.

Three steps in front of the glass entrance of the office building, one of the four security guards blocked his path.

Though the man was wearing sunglasses, despite the fact that there was no sun, the inspector recognized him.

Just a few years earlier he had appeared on television, on the TeleVigàta channel, to tell the story of his services as a private contractor in Iraq. He was built like a tank, with red hair.

'Where do you think you're going?'

And he made the mistake of putting a hand on Montalbano's chest. The inspector looked first at the guard's hand, then in his eyes.

'One . . .' he said.

'What's that supposed to mean?'

'It means that when I get to three I'm going to crush your balls,' the inspector said ever so calmly.

And he smiled at him with affection, like a brother.

The guard jerked his hand away as if he'd burnt it. And he stepped aside.

*

There wasn't a soul inside the office building. But a fancy sign in the lobby provided all the directions necessary. The president's offices were on the top floor. Montalbano took the lift.

He came out in a waiting room that looked made for a hotel for Arab sheiks. Apparently the more tasteless something is, the more expensive. There were two desks with a great many telephones and computers on them. The chairs behind them, however, were vacant. A young man of about thirty with the surly attitude typical of bodyguards was standing near a window. As soon as he saw Montalbano, he came towards him, but the inspector noticed an open door on the left and went through it.

The room was as big as a dance hall, and the president's desk was in proportion to this. Sitting in a swivelling, reclining, pivoting, climate-controlled armchair that could probably fly, if necessary, sat a man of about forty, well groomed, well dressed, well conditioned, and well cologned.

But Giovanni Trincanato was, above all, disagreeable from the moment one set eyes on him. Irredeemably obnoxious, in fact, in a way that did not allow for any softening of opinion over time.

Mimì Augello, sunk deep inside an armchair from which he might never be able to extract himself again, was looking at a magazine.

Seeing the inspector come in, Trincanato asked: 'And who are you?'

'Inspector Montalbano, police.'

Trincanato stood up and came towards the inspector, holding his hand out.

'Pleased to meet you. Trincanato's the name.'

He grasped Montalbano's hand and, still holding it, asked:

'Have you managed yet to get him the hell out of here?'

'Who?'

'The arsehole who hanged himself.'

In a flash, Montalbano's hand slipped from the man's grasp, flew through the air, struck Trincanato's face with force, then withdrew just as fast, grabbed the man's hand again, and shook it as if it had never left.

Mimì's eyes didn't have the time to transmit clearly to his brain what they'd just seen.

But his ears, on the other hand, had for their part registered the classic *crack!* of a serious, proper slap.

'Pleased to meet you,' said Montalbano, smiling cordially and releasing Trincanato's hand.

Then he turned his back and left the room.

TWO

Trincanato stood there mesmerized, paralysed, and incredulous, still holding his hand out.

If he didn't feel half his face still smarting, he wouldn't even have known he'd been slapped.

He looked over at Augello as though asking him to explain what had just happened.

Had he been smacked or not?

But Augello returned his gaze with the innocent expression of an angel just descended from heaven.

And so Trincanato decided that perhaps the moment had come to get a sudden toothache.

And since the inspector was still smiling as he left the building, the 'contractor', seeing him, hopped to one side to let him pass.

'I'm going to the station,' he said to Fazio.

He took two steps and came back.

'Has anyone informed the family?'

'Well, Chief, I told Trincanato to do it, but he just said it wasn't up to him.'

If the inspector had known this earlier, in addition to the smack, he would have thrown in a kick to Trincanato's balls, just for good measure.

'And so?'

'And so I sent Galluzzo with a squad car to take care of it. That way, if any family member wants to see the body . . .'

'You did the right thing, Fazio. See you later.'

*

He spent a good hour signing papers that were steadily fed to him by Sergeant Genuardi, not bothering even to look at them. He would merely write his first and last names in the spot where the sergeant was pointing, then stare off into the empty space outside the door to his office.

At a certain point, from the depths of that nothingness Catarella appeared in the hallway, walking rather strangely.

He was approaching stiffly, mechanically, sort of like a cross between a robot and a sleepwalker, his eyes like saucers.

Genuardi also noticed him.

'What's up with Catarella? He looks like he's on drugs.'

Catarella came through the doorway and kept advancing in a straight line until his knees knocked against the side of the desk. Only then did his eyes focus on the inspector.

He looked around and broke into a beatific smile. 'You feel OK, Cat?'

''Sgré . . . great, Chief.'

'Anything wrong?'

'Jess gimme a seccun' to c'leck m'self . . . Iss not easy to talk . . .'

He gulped, took a deep breath, opened his mouth, made no sound, closed it, and waved his right arm five times in a circular motion to show extreme wonder.

'Jeez, 'a'ss somthin'!'

'What's something!'

'What a goil, Chief!'

'A woman?'

'Yeah, Chief. A goil woman! Gidazzlin' as the sun! Iss only inna movies ya see 'em like 'at!'

'Where'd you see her?'

'Righ' 'ere onna premisses, Chief, righ' 'ere!'

He said this in a kind of wail, simultaneously stamping his feet as if he needed to pee.

'And what's she want?'

'She says she was violenced.'

Montalbano leapt out of his chair. 'Where?'

'In a li'l street jess behin' the ol' choich.'

'When?'

''Bout half a 'our ago.'

'Then the first thing we have to do is have her examined by a doctor. Genuardi, you take care of it.'

Genuardi set off at a run but then stopped in his tracks when Catarella cried out in confusion:

'Bu' wha'ss a dacter for, Chief? It was nuttin'.'

'What do you mean, it was nothing? You said she was raped! Violated!'

'Raped? Violatered? I said 'at?'

'You said it just now, Cat!'

'I did?'

'Yes, you did!' Montalbano and Genuardi chimed in duet.

'Nah, Chief, I said "violenced",' Catarella muttered. 'She was rabbed wit' violence.'

Genuardi and Montalbano looked at each other and rolled their eyes.

Catarella's face turned red, but he said nothing. Hanging his head and staring at the floor, he beat his fist against his chest as if to say mea culpa.

'Can I come in?' asked Augello, poking his head inside the door.

His timing was perfect.

'Mimì, here's a case tailor-made for you. There's an unusually beautiful girl—'

'Where?' asked Augello, one foot already raised, about to break into a run.

'I set 'er down inna waitin' room,' said Catarella.

Mimì literally disappeared in the twinkling of an eye.

*

Enzo, the trattoria owner and its only waiter, bent down to speak softly into Montalbano's ear.

'You know, Inspector, with all this bad weather, none of the fishing boats is putting out.'

The inspector felt his heart give a tug. But then he saw two other customers eating fish.

'What about the fillets of sole those people are eating?'

'Frozen.'

He had to resign himself. 'So what can you bring me?'

'Inspector, I've got *pasta alla carrittera,* and for the main course, an aubergine Parmigiana that's—'

'Sounds good.'

From the very first forkful he realized he wasn't missing a thing, and that a break from the usual fish menu was a welcome change. To the point that he said to Enzo: 'Bring me another helping of aubergine.'

At that moment Mimì came into the trattoria with a girl of about twenty, at least five foot ten, but with legs a good ten feet long, hair so blonde it looked white, blue eyes, and a face that seemed familiar to the inspector.

She was wearing a pair of jeans so tight that they looked more like the skin on a fruit than fabric.

More than beautiful, she was stunning, impressive.

And most certainly American. Only on the American prairies did they raise girls like that, probably on a diet of popcorn, Coca-Cola, and Texas steaks. Then they spiffed them up with a coat of brightly coloured enamel and put them on the market.

Mimì coolly waved *ciao-ciao,* and the inspector replied in kind.

What men of the world they were!

The couple sat down at the table in front of Montalbano's. Augello had his back to him.

Enzo brought the aubergine. He was breathing heavily and unable to take his eyes off the girl.

'*Matre santa,* what a woman! Where did Inspector Augello catch that phenomenon of nature?'

Then he went over to their table.

'What would you two like to order?'

'Have you got any fresh fish?'

'Fresh as you want.'

Enzo was on solid ground. He was aware Augello didn't know the first thing about fish. You could serve him a three-thousand-year-old fish extracted from the polar ice cap and he would think it was the day's catch.

Mimì turned to the girl and asked her something in English.

So the inspector'd been right on the money! She was American!

And all at once, he recognized her: She was Barbie!

An equestrian Barbie; more precisely, the one in the display window of Mrs Ersilia Rocca's toy shop on the main street.

He put his head down and resumed eating.

When he was done, he had to restrain himself from asking for a third helping. It might look bad.

Getting up, he cast a glance over at Mimì's table.

They were deep in English conversation. Augello's hand was halfway across the table, with Barbie's hand resting on top.

*

A light rain was falling. The inspector didn't feel much like taking his customary stroll along the jetty to the lighthouse.

He slipped into his car, which he'd made Gallo go and get for him, and drove off in the direction of home. The gloomy day had made him a little sleepy. An hour or so in the dark would do him good.

When he went into the bathroom to get undressed, he found it flooded. The water had even invaded the bedroom, and was still pouring out of the tap Adelina had opened and forgotten about.

It was feast or famine, in his house: drought or flood. No middle path.

He turned off the tap, went into the cupboard, found a stack of old newspapers, opened each page and laid them down on the floor to absorb the water. When they were soaked, he picked them back up, rolled them into a ball, and threw them into the bin.

Then he took a couple of dry mops and sopped up the remaining water.

When he finished, he looked at the clock and saw that it had taken him a whole hour. The hour he had wanted to devote to napping. He didn't feel sleepy anymore, though. The physical effort had made him quite lucid.

But then he realized that all this wonderful lucidity was of no use to him. He didn't even have a case on his hands.

What was wrong with that?

He'd lately been feeling less and less like working, and now that he had no work, he was complaining?

To dispel the bad mood that descended on him every time the thought of getting old entered his head, he decided to play a practical joke on Augello.

Surely Mimì, not having gone home for lunch, had told Beba, his wife, that he was busy at the police station. And Montalbano was certain that, at that very moment, he was having a ball with the American girl.

So he decided to make a little trouble for him by giving him a ring.

As his hand hovered over the receiver, however, doubt took him.

Did he just want to play a joke on him, or did he want to take revenge on him for being young and always having success with women? No, he decided, he just wanted to have fun.

Was he sure? He was sure. He dialled the number.

'Hello?' Mimì answered.

Montalbano hung up, flustered. He was expecting – as was logical – Beba to answer the phone. So what was Mimì doing at home? Had he not taken things to their logical conclusion?

There were only two possibilities: either the frozen fish had given him a stomach ache, or they'd made a date for that evening.

He lolled about the house for another hour, not knowing what to do, then got bored and went back to the office.

*

'Is Inspector Augello in?'

'Yeah, 'e's onna premisses, Chief.'

'Tell him to come to my office.'

Mimì appeared at once, came in, and sat down.

'How'd it go with the American girl?'

'In general or specifically?'

'As you prefer.'

'Then I'll tell you everything from the beginning. First of all, she – her name is Joan, but I didn't quite get her last name – she didn't actually come to us to report a robbery, even though she was in fact robbed.'

'Oh, really? Then why?'

'Because an outrage had been committed against an American citizen.'

'Outrage?'

'You know what these Americans are like. The moment you touch 'em, they fall to pieces.'

'Well, I certainly wouldn't want to defend the culprit,' said Montalbano, 'but a purse-snatcher can't really tell the difference between an American, Swedish, or Dutch girl. He just runs up behind her, reaches out with one hand, and—'

'Exactly. He reaches out with one hand.'

'Explain.'

'The outrage, according to what Joan told me, lies in the fact that the snatcher – who was sitting behind an accomplice who was driving the scooter – as he was reaching out with one hand to snatch her purse, reached down with the other hand and had the audacity to touch her arse.'

'A crime of lèse-majesté, apparently,' said Montalbano. 'And what did you say to her?'

'I said that we, as policemen, weren't really in a position

to do anything about it, and she should turn to the consulate for help.'

'There's an American consulate in Vigàta?'

'I don't know. But there probably is. Maybe up on some desolate cliff overlooking the sea.'

'Mimì, could it be that you've become just a wee bit anti-American?'

'Me?! Come on! I'm the only one on the entire police force who chews original US-brand chewing gum! And I smoke Camels! And I drink Coca-Cola! And I haven't missed a single Schwarzenegger movie! What the hell is wrong with you?'

'OK, OK. Go on.'

'Anyway, I advised the girl not to turn it into a diplomatic incident. Given, also, the delicacy of the reason. I was just joking, of course, but she understood and got rather miffed. She told me she'd been named Miss Dallas just two years ago, and that her derrière was insured for a million dollars.'

'I'd like to read the details of a contract like that,' said Montalbano.

Then he asked: 'But did she file a report for robbery or not?'

'When I asked her if she wanted to, she got all flustered and told me to hold on a second. And she got up, pulled her phone out of the pocket of her jeans, spoke in a soft voice, and then told me it was probably better if she didn't.'

'Why?'

'Dunno.'

'But didn't she have her documents in her handbag?'

'No, she'd left them at the hotel.'

'Odd.'

'And she didn't have much money in it, either. And the handbag was old to boot. In short, based on what she said to me, it wasn't worth the trouble.'

'And how did you end up taking her to Enzo's?'

'Listen, Salvo, if it was up to me I wouldn't have taken her anywhere.'

'Why, didn't you like her?'

'Didn't you see what she looks like? She's a life-size Barbie doll. I like real women. It was she who asked me to invite her to lunch, since she didn't have a cent on her. What could I say? Before we went out, she asked for the name and address of the restaurant we'd be eating at. So I gave them to her, and she called someone on her phone. I thought she was talking maybe to a girlfriend at the hotel.'

'And instead?'

'Well, here's the deal. As we were eating, she filled me in on what she did for a living.'

'Modelling?'

'Only sporadically. That's not her real profession.'

'And what is?'

'Once upon a time they were called whores, but now they're called escorts. Joan is a super-high-class escort. Twelve grand a pop.'

'Really?'

'Negotiable, naturally.'

'So why was she stroking your hand? Did she really think you were that rich?'

'No, she was merely repaying me the equivalent, in her estimation, of the cost of the meal. She was well aware that the only way I could give her twelve thousand euros would be to take out a loan. If you ask me, when Joan came to the station, it wasn't because she felt offended; she was just upset the purse-snatcher had copped a feel for free, without coughing up so much as a single euro.'

'And then what?'

'And then somebody we know came in and took her away with him.'

'Someone we know?'

'Yes indeed. Giovanni Trincanato. Speaking of whom, did you slap him around the head or not?'

'I'd rather leave you in a state of doubt on the question, Mimì. But wait a second. So, was it Trincanato who convinced her not to report the incident?'

'I think so.'

'But what did it matter to him?'

'Dunno . . . maybe he was worried his name might crop up. With the factory shut down and the workers enraged, he certainly wouldn't want word to get around that he'd sent away for such an expensive hooker . . . Maybe he was just being careful.'

'Careful? Trincanato? You must be joking.'

THREE

'Can I come in?' asked Fazio.

'Yeah, come on in. So you're only getting back now?'

'Chief, would you believe it if I told you I didn't even have time to eat lunch?'

'Where were you?'

'Still at Trincanato's.'

'Did something happen?'

'First, two of Spagnolo's kids came. Spagnolo was the worker who hanged himself. But the guards didn't want to let them into the shed.'

'Are they minors?'

'No way! One's thirty, the other's twenty-eight. Both without jobs. Sacked. At any rate, things could have got out of hand if we hadn't been there . . .'

'And then what?'

'And then, when the prosecutor and Dr Pasquano were finished and the body was taken away, Giurlanno, Spagnolo's oldest son, stayed behind and talked with his dad's friends.'

'What was he saying?'

'I don't know, I didn't hear. He was speaking softly. But I could tell the situation was changing. At first they'd all seemed grief-stricken, but now they were starting to get pissed off. And at that exact moment, Trincanato's car came out of the office building's garage with him at the wheel.'

'What time do you think it was?'

'I dunno, maybe around two-thirty.'

Montalbano and Augello looked at each other. Trincanato was clearly going out to pick up the American girl at the trattoria.

A phone rang. Mimì dug one out of his pocket and brought it to his ear. Then he stood up.

'Excuse me a minute,' he said. And he left the room.

'Go on,' Montalbano said to Fazio.

'All of a sudden the workers rushed towards the car to try and stop it, and at the same time the guards hurried over to protect it. But Trincanato stepped on the accelerator and got away, practically running one guy over in the process. Both groups were running so fast towards each other that they inevitably clashed and came to blows.'

'Are you telling me they were unable to stop in time? That there was no aggression on the part of the workers?'

'Chief, that's what it seemed like to me, at least at the start of the scuffle. After, well, you know how it is . . .'

'No, I don't know how it is. You tell me.'

'One guy says one thing, another guy raises a hand, and the whole thing snowballs from there . . .'

'And you didn't intervene?'

'Chief, given the clear disparity between the sides . . .' said Fazio, dodging the question.

Montalbano glared at him.

Fazio looked down.

'Tell me the truth,' the inspector ordered him.

'Come on, Chief, wasn't it better to let the workers blow off a little steam?'

'But the guards were armed! They could have shot somebody!'

'Chief, the first thing the workers did was disarm them. Then Gallo and Galluzzo got them to hand the guns to them.'

'OK, I see. Are you going to tell me when you decided to intervene?'

'At the end.'

'At the end of what?'

'The dustup.'

'You mean when the guards were so battered with punches and kicks that they were on the ground and could no longer get up?'

'More or less. The guy in the worst shape was the ex-contractor. But when I asked him if I should call an ambulance, he said no. He was afraid to lose face, I think.'

'Did you give them back their guns?'

'Yeah. And so they went to get themselves bandaged up, and we guarded the establishment until a new shift of security guards arrived. And now, with your permission, I'd like to go home and get some rest.'

'Go ahead. I'll see you tomorrow.'

*

Naturally, Adelina didn't find any fresh fish at the market, either. So she made him three beef cutlets *alla pizzaiola* and a large platter of caponata.

A day of earthy, rustic stuff.

He ate in the kitchen. It had stopped raining a good while earlier, but it was too chilly on the veranda.

Then he sat in the armchair in front of the television.

He tuned in to TeleVigàta, which was the local TV station that was always loyal to the government, no matter who was in power.

At that moment, the number-one commentator, Pippo Ragonese, was talking. Ragonese had a purse-lipped face that looked like a chicken's arse, and bore a deadly personal grudge against Montalbano.

> *To the already rather long list of businesses in crisis in the Montelusa area, we can now add the Trincanato works in Vigàta. To a superficial observer, the picture may appear indeed unsettling, but the situation is not quite so dramatic as the opposition would have us believe. Of course, the crisis – which is not only Italian, mind you, but global – is real. And we see it everywhere. But just yesterday our Prime Minister, when speaking to a group of industrialists from the Veneto, reminded us of what the government has already done, and announced a series of new measures to be adopted in the coming months. 'I am here to give you all an injection of confidence,' said the head of the government, specifying –*

You can go and give your injection of confidence to Carmine Spagnolo's dead body, thought Montalbano, changing the channel.

He stumbled upon a spy film.

He'd never been able to understand a thing in these spy plots, which were always so complicated. This time he couldn't even work out who'd won and who'd lost, and so he changed channels again, tuning in to the other local television station, the Free Channel, whose news service was directed by a friend of his, Nicolò Zito.

And it was in fact Nicolò who was talking to the camera. He was saying that a month earlier his news programme had reported that a charter flight experienced a rough landing at Nairobi airport in Kenya, leaving some twenty people injured.

There were two things about this story that had aroused Nicolò Zito's curiosity: The first was that sixteen of the injured were Sicilian; and the second was that the aeroplane, which had landed on a Friday evening, was supposed to depart again on Monday morning with the same passengers.

How odd! So you fly all the way to Kenya just to spend Saturday and Sunday there?

He'd conducted an investigation and discovered that there were special round-trip package deals, with all included – flight, meals, and lodging – for certain tourists who weren't going there to visit the country's much-heralded national parks.

Upon arrival at the airport, the passengers would be boarded onto a bus and taken out of town to a special hotel. It wasn't really a proper hotel, but a big casino where people played for high stakes, and it featured restaurants and rooms for eating and sleeping.

In short, whoever came in on those flights would remain shut inside the casino for forty-eight hours straight, gambling all day and all night.

Montalbano turned the TV off and started thinking about what he'd just heard. Since there was a legal limit to the amount of money one could take out of the country, how did these gamblers have such huge sums of cash available? There must have been some kind of banking connection . . .

The phone rang. It was Livia.

The moment he heard her voice, he was overcome by the desire to have her beside him.

'Why don't you come down for a few days?'

'Salvo, you have no idea how much I would like to. But I don't dare ask for a single day off.'

'Have you got a lot of work?'

'I wish!'

'Then what is it?'

'The situation is really dire here. They're not expecting any more commissions. If I leave my chair vacant for even one day, it will remain vacant forever. They'll fire me. They've already laid off half the employees. You can't imagine how sad it is around here.'

'Maybe you need an injection of confidence from our Prime Minister.'

'Fuck off!' said Livia.

'Me?' asked Montalbano.

But Livia had already hung up.

*

He found himself sitting at the roulette table in the Kenyan casino. He'd spent two days and two nights gambling and losing.

He knew he'd already lost his shirt by that point. He'd squandered two hundred thousand euros, and all he had left were three cards for five hundred.

He took one and was about to wager it.

'We don't accept bets for less than a thousand euros,' said the croupier, who was Joan, the American Barbie.

He gambled all three cards and lost.

'If you're unable to keep playing, please leave the table so someone else can,' Joan ordered him.

He stood up, feeling embarrassed, and was seized by the arm by two burly men.

'You come with us.'

'Where?'

'You have to undergo the treatment reserved for losing players. House rules.'

They took him into a room with a huge desk and a man sitting behind it.

The man stood up and came towards him. He recognized him.

It was Trincanato.

'How much did he lose?' he asked one of the two bouncers.

'Two hundred grand.'

'That means twenty slaps,' said Trincanato. And he delivered the first of them.

Which woke him up in a frothing rage.

But he calmed down at once, seeing that it was a bright, beautiful day without a breath of wind.

He got up, drank some coffee, and went into the bathroom.

Now that it was no longer raining, the water poured out of the shower head like there was no tomorrow.

*

'Ah, Chief, Chief! Ahh, Chief!' Catarella intoned.

Bad sign. Whenever Catarella sang that litany, it meant the commissioner had called.

'What did he want?' asked Montalbano.

'Hizzoner the C'mishner wannit a talk t'yiz poissonally in poisson all oigentlike an' immimediately!'

'Any news?'

'Where?'

'Here, at the station.'

'Nah, Chief, nuttin'.'

'Then I'm on my way.'

He went out to his car, got in, and drove off.

A phone call from Hizzoner the C'mishner almost always meant threats, scoldings, dressing-downs . . .

This time, however, his conscience was clear, among other reasons because nothing whatsoever had happened in Vigàta for the past month.

He had the good fortune not to run into Dr Lattes, the chief of the commissioner's cabinet, in the waiting room. Lattes, known to subordinates as Lattes e Mieles, was convinced the inspector was married with children. The commissioner had even explained to him that Montalbano was a bachelor, but the man held fast to his idée fixe, and there was no changing his mind.

Commissioner Bonetti-Alderighi received the inspector at once.

Wearing a dark frown on his face, he didn't say hello, didn't gesture for him to sit down, but only raised his eyes for an instant and then looked back down at the papers in front of him.

Since the mood was one of open battle, the inspector sat down just the same, pulled out his handkerchief, and blew his nose with a honk remarkably similar to the horn of an HGV.

Bonetti-Alderighi looked up as though irritated.

'Sorry, I've got a bad cold,' said the inspector, putting his handkerchief down on the desk.

It was a calculated move. The commissioner was a cleanliness freak and obsessively afraid of being infected with any illness whatsoever. And now he would be anxious to get rid of Montalbano as quickly as possible. Which proved to be the case.

'I sent for you because I received a complaint against you today.'

'Against me?!'

'More precisely, against several members of your force.'

'Mind telling me who filed the complaint?'

'The president of Securitas.'

'Is that some kind of insurance company?'

'Stop playing stupid, Montalbano. Securitas hires out private security guards.'

'May I ask a question?'

'Go ahead.'

'Do private security guards technically have jurisdiction over public safety? I honestly don't know.'

The commissioner himself probably didn't know, either, and therefore became irritated.

'That's not the point! In the complaint it is stated that no fewer than six security guards in the service of Trincanato in Vigàta were beaten up by workers who were protest—'

'I'm sorry, but are the guards Catholic?' Montalbano asked, interrupting him.

Bonetti-Alderighi hesitated a moment. 'What's that got to do with anything?'

'Well, since you said the workers were Protestants, I was just thinking that . . . you know, like in Ireland, between Catholics and Protestants . . .'

'For the love of God, Montalbano! Stop talking nonsense!'

'I'm sorry, but—'

'Quiet! Those guards were severely beaten by the workers, and your men, who were right there, stood by and did not intervene. So now you must explain why—'

'Can't you see that my question was relevant?' asked Montalbano.

'What question?' asked the commissioner, confused.

'As to whether they had jurisdiction over public safety. Aside from the fact that they're lying, they should have no jurisdiction over what the police do or do not do.'

'I really don't understand what . . .'

Montalbano stood up, assumed an air of indignation, and raised his arm halfway as they did at Pontida.

'Mr Commissioner! That complaint is a lie! And I would add that, given the fact that security guards do not have jurisdiction over any incident involving public safety, they were infringing on the prerogatives of the police, and by adding falsehood to an abuse of power, they—'

'Listen, Montalbano . . .'

'Please allow me, Mr Commissioner, to express the outrage I feel over this act of perfidy!'

'Come now, Montalbano, such harsh words . . .'

'My men were extremely brave to fight against such overwhelming forces! Do you realize that? Three against fifty!'

'But who were these fifty?'

'The other workers, Mr Commissioner. Who wanted to intervene in the clash between some twenty of their workmates and the security guards. If they'd entered the fray, the guards would never have made it out alive! But my men prevented that from happening. Of course, they couldn't very well keep fifty protesters at bay and at the same time go and help the six arseho . . . I mean, the six guards!'

He collapsed in his chair, exhausted, grabbed the handkerchief, blew his nose – this time sounding more like a steam engine going uphill – knitted his eyebrows, and started opening and closing his mouth as though about to sneeze.

Alarmed, the commissioner dismissed him. 'Go, just go – I'll clear everything up myself.'

*

He took his time driving back to Vigàta, puttering along at about thirty kilometres an hour, enjoying the landscape.

It didn't take long before a queue of cars formed behind him. Horns began to blare, since there was a double line in the middle of the road, prohibiting passing.

But he didn't give a flying fuck, and kept on driving at thirty.

Then the road widened, and all the cars behind him overtook him, releasing a tsunami of insults ('idiot!' 'deadbeat!' 'cretin!') as they passed.

The only car that didn't make it in time was a shiny black Mercedes that had to remain behind him. The driver started honking like a madman.

The inspector was certain that if the guy had had a gun he would have shot him.

He looked at him in the rear-view mirror. It was a military man.

As he got a better look, however, he realized that the hat the man was wearing was not military, as he'd thought, but a chauffeur's cap. And the cut of the jacket's shoulders was also that of a chauffeur. Maybe the man even wore gaiters, the way they used to do.

At that moment the driver of the Mercedes decided to pass him, even though he couldn't.

Seeing the guy lurch way out to the left and accelerate, the inspector instinctively swerved to the right as another car came barrelling fast towards them in the other lane.

He closed his eyes and heard some tyres screeching, and then his car stopped. When he was able again to resume contact with the world, he was certain that his car, luckily, had not been damaged.

He'd gone off the road at a spot where the ditch was paved over, and had continued for a few more yards, ending up under an almond tree.

He got out and realized that the Mercedes, too, had ended up off the road on the other side.

Despite the rain of the previous days, the ground was still fairly firm, and the tyres hadn't sunk into the mud. A simple manoeuvre would suffice to get him out of that pickle.

He waited for a let-up in the flow of traffic, then crossed the road.

But then he stopped and didn't take another step, because right there in front of him was a veritable swamp. And he didn't want to get his shoes dirty.

The driver of the Mercedes was in full chauffeur's livery. Even the boots. He was talking on his mobile.

Montalbano was sure he was calling a rescue service, since the wheels of his car were half sunken in mud.

The inspector decided it was best to drop the whole thing, and turned around to go back to his car.

FOUR

'Just a minute, please, sir!'

He stopped and turned around. It was the chauffeur, coming towards him.

He was a big, strapping man, the kind who inspires fear, and he walked like an ogre in a children's story, because with every step he took he had to raise his gaitered leg to free it from the mud into which it was sinking. And each step went *plof, plof*.

The inspector braced himself defensively.

If the man wanted to start a fight and sucker-punched him, he would surely break the inspector's face into many little pieces. Montalbano therefore stood firm on his feet and bowed his head slightly: if the man assumed a threatening air he would headbutt him à la Zidane – it was his only hope. A punch wouldn't even faze the guy.

But once the man was standing in front of him, he gave a sort of half bow and doffed his cap.

'I apologize for the accident. The fact is that I'm really in a hurry. I'm so sorry.'

'That's all right,' said the inspector, taken by surprise. The last thing he was expecting was an act of contrition.

'Was your car badly damaged?'

'No, it's not damaged at all.'

'Can it be moved?'

'Yes.'

'If you'll give me the keys, I'll put it back on the road for you, to spare you the trouble.'

What, did this ogre belong to some kind of Boy Scouts association? Always doing good deeds, and helping nice old folks in trouble?

'Thank you. The keys are in the ignition.'

The man was quite competent, and five minutes later the car was idling at the side of the road and ready to go.

'Could you do me a favour?' the chauffeur asked.

'What do you need?' asked Montalbano, grateful to him for having spared him the effort of manoeuvring the car.

'Are you by any chance going into Vigàta?'

'Yes.'

'Could you give the young lady a lift into town? I have to wait here for the breakdown lorry.'

He hadn't noticed that there was a passenger in the Mercedes. That would have been difficult, though, since the car had darkly tinted windows.

'Of course.'

'You're very kind. Thank you so much.'

Not even in China were they so courteous.

Montalbano stood there watching the chauffeur go

back across the road, reach the Mercedes, open the rear door, bend down, pick the woman up, and, still holding her in his arms the way they say a newly wed groom is supposed to do with his bride, come back towards the road.

She must be some sort of poor paralytic . . . thought the inspector.

But when, after crossing the muddy area, the chauffeur set the woman on her feet, Montalbano practically gasped for air. It was as if he was simultaneously heart-struck and punched in the stomach.

Some paralytic!

If anything, she had the power to paralyse anyone who laid eyes on her!

As a case in point, at the mere sight of her, the queue of cars suddenly began to waver, slow down, and drift left of centre or off the road. When she started to cross the road, the traffic came to a halt on both sides, opening like the waters of the Red Sea at Moses's approach.

She looked about twenty, like Joan, and was as tall as Joan, but, unlike the American, she had very curly jet-black hair, a dusky complexion, a mouth that had the same effect as a red traffic light, and a pair of big, sparkly, dark dark eyes.

Her legs, too, were ten feet long, and, as if that wasn't enough, she was wearing a miniskirt up to her crotch.

'The young lady doesn't speak Italian,' said the driver. 'Just Spanish and English.'

'Carmencita,' said the girl, holding her hand out to him.

He should have known.

Montalbano refrained from saying *olé!* but merely shook Carmencita's hand. She replied with a broad smile.

She had the teeth of someone who eats raw meat.

From the road came the sounds of screeching halts, crashing metal, and insults as fierce as they were imaginative. It was best to get the girl out of sight as quickly as possible, otherwise she might cause injury and death.

'Please have a seat,' said the inspector, opening the car door for her.

The girl sat down.

The flow of traffic resumed its normal speed.

'Thank you,' said the chauffeur. 'You should take the young lady to the home of Mr Giovanni Trincanato. Do you know him?'

'How could I not?' said Montalbano.

The girl's miniskirt, now that she was seated, was practically at her armpits.

Trying hard not to look in that direction, Montalbano launched into a litany of curses in his head as he put the car in gear.

What kind of babe addiction did that great big son of a bitch Trincanato have, anyway?

Then, after they'd been driving along for barely five minutes and were just another five from the first buildings on the edge of town, it was their bad luck to run into a carabinieri checkpoint.

There were three cars ahead of the inspector's, but they worked things out fast. There was a lance corporal leaning against the carabinieri squad car, and two officers conducting the checks. Montalbano didn't recognize any of them.

'Good morning. Licence and registr . . .' said one of the two officers, leaning down into the window but suddenly losing the power of speech at the sight of Carmencita's luminous and entirely exposed thighs.

'Did you mean to say "registration"?' A mildly nervous Montalbano helped him out.

But the poor officer seemed to be suffering a heart attack, eyes bulging and face beetroot-red. He was even trembling a little.

Meanwhile another carabiniere had come up to the window and bent down.

And, naturally, he, too, opened his eyes wide and turned red as a turkey.

'. . . and registration!' said the first officer, having recovered the power of speech.

Montalbano handed them to him, and the carabiniere moved reluctantly away from the window.

The other officer joined him, and they began an intense discussion, occasionally looking over at the inspector.

'You boss?' Carmencita asked him excitedly, putting one hand on his leg and squeezing it gently.

A cold shudder went up Montalbano's spine.

Then the first carabiniere returned and bent down. 'Is the young lady your daughter?' he asked, giving him back his documents.

Daughter? It was a double insult: the man was not only

telling him he was old, but that he had a slut for a daughter. Montalbano suddenly saw red and went wild:

'What the hell is it to you?'

'Don't raise your voice!'

'I'll raise whatever I feel like raising!'

'Your insurance is expired and you have a broken rear light!' the second carabiniere chimed, to back him up.

'Get out of the car!' ordered the first one.

Montalbano opened the door, got out, and started running.

'Stop!' said the first carabiniere, taking up his assault rifle.

But by now Montalbano was right in front of the lance corporal, who had noticed that things had taken a bad turn. The inspector was trembling in rage. But he decided to put on a little show. He spoke very fast to the young man, and in a soft voice: 'Sbaram sess shtipp tooty pooty,' he said, panting heavily.

The corporal hesitated, apparently thinking he was dealing with a nutcase.

'Please calm down,' he said. 'What did you say?'

'It's the password! Answer!'

'Who *are* you, anyway?'

'Inspector Montalbano, Vigàta Police, but momentarily on a mission for the CFRB. Here's my badge.'

He pulled it out and handed it to him.

'Now give me the counterpassword, for the love of God!'

'Listen, Inspector . . .'

Montalbano pretended to be overcome by doubt. 'Are you Lance Corporal Corridoni?'

'No.'

'Then there's been a terrible mistake! My God, what a disaster! Let me go at once!'

'Paganelli, let him through!' the lance corporal ordered the carabiniere with the rifle, looking lost at sea.

Montalbano turned around, got back in the car, and drove off.

And in the ten minutes it took to reach Trincanato's house he went through the torments of hell, as Carmencita did nothing but caress him and rub against him, by now convinced that he was a powerful crime boss.

*

'Ah, Chief!'

'What is it?'

'I wannit a tell yiz 'atta minnit ya left fer Montelusa, yer cleanin' leddy Adelina called.'

'And wha'd she want?'

'She tol' me to tell yiz 'at she's rilly sorry, bu' she's incapacitated as to cummin to yer 'ouse, in so much as she – she bein' 'er, an' 'er bein' Adelina – 's gat a li'l fever.'

A proper pain in the arse. This meant there wouldn't be any dinner waiting for him at home that evening. And he didn't like going out twice to the trattoria in a single day.

'Augello in?'

'Yeah, 'e's onna premisses.'

'Tell him to come to my office.'

When he'd finished telling him the story of Carmencita, leaving out the part about the carabinieri roadblock, Mimì said: 'So you had another chance to see Trincanato!'

'Unfortunately I didn't have the pleasure, because the front door was locked, and I left the girl out there, waiting for someone to come and open it. So, what do you think?'

'What do you want me to think, Salvo? Around town everyone's always known that Trincanato has two vices: women and gambling. He's a legal adult and unmarried, so who's he supposed to answer to?'

'Well, to his workers, for starters . . . Maybe not all of them, that would be too many, but at least to the family of the man who hanged himself.'

'Oh, give me a break!' exclaimed Mimì, getting up and going back into his office.

Fazio came in.

'Chief, there's something I wanted to tell you.'

'So tell me.'

'I dropped in at the Trincanato plant this morning to check out the situation.'

'And so?'

'There were only five workers there holding down the fort. One of them said to me they'd taken a collection for Spagnolo's funeral.'

'Tell me something: did Trincanato make a contribution?'

'Absolutely! He sent twenty euros, which the workers promptly sent back.'

Montalbano felt indignant, rage mounting, but made no comment.

'All quiet, therefore?'

'Too quiet.'

'What do you mean?'

'Exactly what I said. They all seemed too quiet to me.'

'So you're worried they're cooking something up?'

'In all honesty, I don't know what to say.'

'Are the security guards there?'

'Yep.'

'Then let them worry about whether the establishment is in danger or not.'

'Chief, the workers can go wherever they want. When I got there, the guards were removing a banner from the top floor of the office building, which the workers had hung there during the night, though the place was guarded even then. Apparently the guards were asleep, since they didn't notice till the next morning.'

'Did you see what the banner said?'

'Yeah. It said: "We got no money, just mouths to feed /But the boss got all the whores he needs." '

Montalbano weighed his options.

'Listen, Fazio, I wouldn't get involved in this business.'

'I feel the same way. I just thought I should let you know.'

*

He left the station a little earlier than usual to go to the di Donato grocery, which always had excellent but very expensive stuff. He wanted to buy something for dinner, since Adelina wasn't coming.

Going in, he noticed that the customer directly ahead of him was the chauffeur from the Mercedes, who immediately recognized him, brought two fingers to his cap by way of salute, and said: 'Please, after you . . .'

'Thank you, but you were here first.' The guy was still in China, apparently.

The chauffeur pulled a sheet of paper out of his pocket and turned to di Donato.

'Mr Trincanato wanted us to do a checklist.'

'So let's do a checklist!'

'Two legs of prosciutto di Parma, two mortadellas from Bra, Colonnata lard, a whole round of Parmigiano Reggiano, and thirty Camemberts.'

'Got 'em all.'

'Three smoked salmons, forty jars of caviar?'

'Got 'em.'

'Fifty bottles of Veuve Clicquot?'

'Got 'em.'

Montalbano's jaw dropped.

'Good,' said the chauffeur. 'And what about the rest? Bread, pasta, assorted condiments?'

'We've got everything.'

'All right, then I'm off to the butcher's. Somebody will be by around five to pick it all up.'

'OK.'

The chauffeur gave a half bow to Montalbano by way of goodbye, then went out.

The inspector felt almost too embarrassed to ask di Donato for a hundred grams of prosciutto, another hundred of salami, and a small jar of olives in oil.

To save face in the grocer's eyes, he also bought a bottle of Prosecco.

*

'What's wrong, Inspector. Got worries? You're eating without conviction,' said Enzo as Montalbano listlessly brought a forkful of *spaghetti alle vongole* to his lips.

Enzo had guessed right. The inspector was indeed still thinking about that scene in the grocer's shop.

How many women did Trincanato keep in his house, anyway? Did he have a harem or something?

And how long would that stock of food last? Fifteen days? Ten?

Assuming he had, say, five women, that would make six people, including Trincanato himself.

Fifty bottles of champagne meant more than eight bottles a head . . .

Good God! No wonder his company went bankrupt . . .

When he got up from the table, the inspector felt weighted down.

Not because he'd eaten too much, however. Maybe the food had got stuck in his stomach because he was thinking too much about the kind of life Trincanato led.

The only hope was to take a vigorous walk along the jetty.

Reaching the flat rock that lay right below the lighthouse, he sat down and lit a cigarette.

There was the usual crab, which he liked to pester by throwing pebbles at it. This time, however, it noticed him in time and, to avoid being annoyed, slipped nimbly into a hole in the rock.

From where he was sitting, Montalbano had the whole town before him, but when he began to follow the flight of a seagull with his eyes, he turned to the opposite side, towards the mouth of the harbour.

And he was mesmerized.

There was a large sailing ship he'd never seen before, manoeuvring before entering the harbour with its auxiliary engines; it had just finished lowering its sails and was in the process of making a half turn so that the bows faced the mouth of the port.

How light and elegant it was!

For a split-second the inspector saw an unknown flag waving astern.

Moments later the all-white schooner, which looked like a hospital ship, began to pass ever so slowly before him, as if wanting to show itself off in all its beauty.

The name on the bows was *Halcyon*.

Montalbano estimated the ship to be over eighty feet long and almost twenty-five feet wide. With the crew and passengers, it could probably carry up to about thirty people.

From his vantage point he could follow the ship's

manoeuvres as it came alongside a quay near the jetty of his daily strolls.

The man taking the mooring rope and looping it with a slipknot around a bollard was, in fact, the usual solitary fisherman with whom the inspector every so often exchanged a few words.

Moments later a gangway was lowered from the ship to the quay.

A sailor came out and started pacing back and forth in front of the ship, as though waiting for someone.

The deck of the ship was deserted. Not a soul in sight.

Deciding his little break was over, Montalbano got up from the rock and started walking.

When he was about twenty yards from the gangway, he saw a Mercedes approaching at high speed.

He was under the impression it was Trincanato's car, now with all the mud washed off, and without really knowing why, he obeyed his instincts, stopped in his tracks, and hid behind an empty lorry.

The Mercedes pulled up right in front of the gangway. The liveried driver got out and opened the boot.

Meanwhile Barbie and Carmencita had come out of the car.

They shook hands with the chauffeur and boarded the ship, immediately vanishing below decks.

The sailor took two large, fancy-looking suitcases out of the boot and, with the chauffeur's help, carried them up into the schooner.

Montalbano didn't budge. The chauffeur surely wouldn't

be staying long aboard the ship, since he'd left the Mercedes open. And he indeed reappeared less than ten minutes later, got into his car, and drove off.

Only then did the inspector resume his walk.

FIVE

He felt a little bewildered.

He'd made a whole series of conjectures about Trincanato that were probably all wrong.

Those two girls at his house were only passing through, waiting to board the *Halcyon*. In the meantime Trincanato, of course, took advantage of the opportunity; but it was one thing to keep them around for, say, a whole month, and another just to have them there for a short stay.

What sort of relationship, therefore, did Trincanato have with the owner of the schooner?

And why did they need two deluxe escorts on board?

There was something that didn't add up.

*

It wasn't until around half-past four, as he was signing papers, that the scene in the grocer's shop came back into his mind. He kept on signing for another ten minutes, then told Genuardi he had something to attend to, went out, got in his car, drove off, and fifteen minutes later was pulling up outside di Donato's grocery.

Not wanting to give the impression that he had the place under surveillance, he got out of the car and started looking in the display window of Vigàta's only bookshop.

About five minutes later a taxi pulled up, and out of it came two sailors wearing T-shirts with the name *Halcyon* on them.

They went into the grocer's and came back out loaded down with packages and big cases of bottles of wine, which they started loading into the boot of the taxi.

The inspector got back in his car and returned to the office. Trincanato was not only in charge of the schooner's guests' sexual needs, but also their stomachs.

Was he doing it as a friendly gesture, or did he gain something from it? He might even be co-owner of the ship; or perhaps he'd rented it to give himself a genuine pleasure cruise.

But, all things considered, what the hell did he, Montalbano, care about the whole thing?

Still . . .

Still, no matter what he did, all the questions he had about Trincanato continued to spin about in his head in the hours that followed, and towards evening he became convinced that if he didn't start coming up with a minimum of answers, he wasn't going to get any sleep that night.

Luckily for him, Fazio came through the door just as he was getting up to go home.

'Where've you been?'

'Chief, for the first part of the afternoon I was out in the country, in the Allegracori district, because they busted into the wrong house looking for Don Ciccino Siragusa . . . Then I had to dash over to the port when a brawl broke out between two trawler crews.'

'Speaking of the port, there's a schooner there, the *Halcyon*, which—'

'There *was* a schooner there.'

'What do you mean?'

'I mean it's gone. Out to sea.'

'But it wasn't here even five hours!'

'That's what it usually does.'

'Usually? You mean it's come here before?'

'Absolutely. It showed up for the first time about six months ago.'

'How come I've never seen it before?'

'Chief, it normally arrives at around seven in the morning, stays for three or four hours, then puts out again. Just long enough to resupply.'

'Resupply with what?'

'Fuel, food—'

'Whores . . .'

Fazio gave him a puzzled look.

'Whores, whores . . .' the inspector insisted.

'Really?'

'I saw them with my own eyes. And do you know who has the honour of serving and supplying the royal house?'

'No.'

'Our very own Trincanato.'

'Really?' Fazio repeated.

'And he's also the ship's storekeeper. He does all the shopping for everyone, crew and guests.'

Fazio began to grasp what Montalbano was getting at. 'Would you like me to gather some information?'

'What do *you* think?'

*

After he'd finished eating, he was looking out at the sea in the night and thinking about how at that moment the passengers of the *Halcyon* must be living it up, when he had an idea.

Surely his old friend Ingrid Sjostrom, who was a member of Montelusa's hedonistic high society, must know Trincanato and his habits. He decided to give it a try, even though he was absolutely positive that Ingrid wouldn't be home at that hour.

'Hullo? Whoodis?'

One of Ingrid's specialities was changing housekeepers every couple of weeks and hiring only people from far-flung lands.

This one must have been from some long-lost island off one of the African coasts.

'This is Montalbano. Is Miss Ingrid at home?'

'No, she not home.'

But Ingrid also had a mobile phone.

'Salvo, what a lovely surprise! To what do I owe this privilege?'

'Is this an OK time to talk?'

'Let's say you have five minutes.'

'Can we meet?'

'Tonight no, tomorrow yes.'

'My place for dinner?'

'All right.'

*

The following morning he found an odd letter among a host of other items on his desk. He didn't know whether to be pleased or displeased.

It had been sent by the personnel office and informed Inspector Salvo Montalbano that, after a thorough examination of their records, they'd found that he had accumulated so many unused days of leave that he could, if he so desired, stay at home as of that moment until the day of his retirement.

Consequently [Oh, how the bureaucrats loved the word 'consequently'!], Inspector Salvo Montalbano should consider himself on leave from the date of reception of this missive, for a period of not less than ten (10) days, in order to commence a gradual diminution of the abovementioned accumulated days of leave. Owing to its urgency, such diminution cannot, under any circumstances, be further delayed. It could, as a general guideline, be maintained in increments of ten (10) days, alternating with two months of time spent at the workplace.

In the event that an ongoing investigation should perchance extend beyond the two months allocated, Inspector Salvo Montalbano would be able, upon request to the appropriate authorities, to obtain an extension of the allotted work time.

He summoned Mimì Augello and got him to read the letter.

'Nice little pain in the arse!' was Augello's comment.

'So you're unhappy you won't be seeing me for ten days every two months?'

'To tell you the truth, Salvo, I would have been happier if it had been the other way around, and you had to work for ten days and then stay away for two months.'

'Well, be happy with what you got.'

'But do you know what the problem is?'

'You tell me.'

'The problem is that for the ten days you're not here, the commissioner will send somebody to run the station.'

'But there's you!'

'Salvo, you know as well as I do that the commissioner thinks of us as a unit, as if we were married. He doesn't distinguish between the two of us.'

'Well, it's clear he's a stupid fuck. There's an abyss of difference between you and me.'

'Let's drop it. But the commissioner will take advantage of the situation to undermine our station. You know what he thinks about us. He even once called us a band of mafiosi.'

Mimì was right.

'If you want, I can go and talk to him.'

'Never mind, that would only make things worse,' said Mimì, going back to his office.

*

'Hey, Cat, I want you to phone me Livia at work.'

'OK, Chief, can I have the number?'

'You mean you don't have it?'

'Nah, Chief, I don'.'

'C'mon, Cat! You've got it on a piece of paper right beside your phone! Home number, office number, mobile . . .'

'Wait a secon', Chief . . . Nah, iss not 'ere!'

Cursing the saints, the inspector got up and went to the switchboard cupboard. Catarella stood at attention.

The piece of paper was right there. Montalbano showed it to him, resting his index finger on it.

'And what, may I ask, is this?'

'Bu', Chief, ya tol' me to phone Milivia, an' so I was lookin' for a Mr Milivia!'

'So what was I supposed to say?'

'If ya juss say: "Call my goilfrenn fer me . . ." '

He finally had Livia on the line.

'What's wrong?' asked Livia, alarmed, since Salvo almost never called her at work.

'Nothing's wrong. But since I'm being forced by the higher-ups to take a ten-day holiday starting today, I thought I'd come and see you in Boccadasse.'

'Damn!'

Such enthusiasm!

'Thank you for that affectionate reply.'

'I wasn't referring to you, silly!'

'Then what is it?'

'The day after tomorrow I have to go away with my boss and Annamaria, his secretary. I was going to tell you this evening.'

'Where are you going?'

'Switzerland, Germany, France . . .'

'How long will you be away?'

'About eight to ten days.'

'So, nothing doing?'

'I'm so sorry . . . But listen. Why don't you come here anyway?'

'To do what?'

'You can do nothing, just the same as you'd do in Vigàta.'

Exchange one nothing for another. It wasn't a bad idea.

But there might be another solution.

'Listen, Livia. I could almost certainly get permission to delay my holiday for a week or more. So I could come up to your place, you'd come back shortly thereafter, and that way we could spend a few days together. What do you think?'

'I think that's an excellent idea.'

He hung up, looked at the signature at the bottom of the letter, and picked the receiver up again.

'Cat, get me Athos Fornaciari at the personnel office.' He was just wondering whether the guy had any friends named Aramis or Porthos, when he heard a commanding voice come over the line.

'Montalbano, before you say anything I should warn you that the letter you received allows for no waivers.'

Should he challenge him to a duel at the Carmelite convent, or play the model employee? He opted for the latter.

'I am eager to comply, sir, believe me.'

'Then what do you want?'

What an obnoxious bastard! Montalbano had to make a great effort not to start insulting him.

'I merely wished to inform you that, unfortunately, the case you were so far-sighted as to anticipate is indeed the case.'

'I don't understand.'

'Well, as would happen to be the case, I have a case on my hands. So I think the hypothetical case you foresaw is indeed the case in this case.'

'Would you please speak a little more clearly?'

'I presently have on my hands a highly sensitive – highly sensitive, I repeat – investigation I can neither interrupt nor entrust to anyone else.'

'I see. And how long do you think it will take to bring it to a close?'

'Seven or eight days, at the most. After which I'll leave on holiday straightaway, as you requested.'

Mr Fornaciari had to think about this for a moment. 'Well, if you can say with assurance . . .'

He'd pulled it off.

*

'I must say you've got a good nose, Chief!'

'Tell me everything.'

'There are some pretty strange things about that *Halcyon*.'

'Did you happen to see what flag it was flying?'

'Bolivian.'

'OK, go on.'

'The first oddity is that whenever it comes alongside, only three sailors ever leave the ship. One remains behind to stand guard over the gangway while the other two shop for provisions. And the sailor guarding the gangway is also the one who handles the refuelling.'

'But surely the Customs Police have spoken to the captain?'

'Of course. I spoke to one of their officers. The captain is Brazilian and a man of few words. The customs agents have always found everything in order on board. The agent I talked to also said they've never seen a single passenger on board.'

'So, to conclude, the *Halcyon* arrives here empty, and the crew do their best to be as invisible as possible.'

'So it seems.'

'But it's absurd for a ship like that to sail about on the open sea without any passengers! It makes no sense! One day of navigation must cost more than my annual salary!'

'You're right.'

'So how do you explain it?'

'Chief, somebody who knows about these things pointed out to me that the stern area has been altered.'

'How?'

'It was widened to twenty-five feet.'

'For what purpose?'

'Maybe to allow a helicopter to land.'

'And what do you think?'

'I think it's possible.'

'So the passengers embark and disembark via helicopter?'

'Why not?'

'But wouldn't it be more logical simply to set up a rendezvous in some port? For example, couldn't the passengers have embarked here in Vigàta, when the *Halcyon* called for provisions?'

'That depends.'

'On what?'

'On who the passengers are.'

'Explain.'

'I've been giving this a lot of thought, Chief. Say two or three well-known rich people, who are friends with one another – I dunno, bankers, or businessmen, or politicians – say these guys want to take a holiday together and live it up, gambling from morning till night, with a couple of beautiful whores and a kilo of cocaine, out of everyone's sight, what better place to do so than on the *Halcyon*? But if they board the ship on land, they risk being recognized. And so they use a helicopter instead.'

'You may be right. But the passenger could also just board at an unknown port where you couldn't find a journalist for love or money.'

'They might do that, too.'

'So,' the inspector concluded, 'the *Halcyon* is presumably a kind of floating gambling den and brothel?'

'Looks that way.'

'Do you know how many people it can carry altogether?'

'Quite a few, I'm sure, because aside from the crew and passengers, there's got to be room for the croupiers, a few chambermaids, and the hookers.'

'It doesn't make sense to me. If it was a brothel, two women wouldn't be enough.'

'That's true. But we don't know that they don't board a few more girls at other ports.'

'Do you know who the owner is?'

'Yes, a Bolivian company. You want me to try to find out more?'

'What for? You've already satisfied my curiosity.'

*

He went and ate at Enzo's, then took his customary walk along the jetty. His fisherman friend was in the usual spot.

'Hello.'

'Hello, Inspector.'

'They biting?'

'Who? I ain't caught nothin' that looks like a fish in two days.'

'Can I bother you for a minute?'

'I'm at your service.'

'Can you tell me anything about that schooner, the *Halcyon*?'

'Sure, Inspector, but what can I really tell you?'

'Well, for example, the other times it came into our port, did it take any women aboard like this time?'

'Yessir. They change girls every fifteen days; they work in half-month shifts, just like in the bordellos.'

'And do they always arrive in the same Mercedes?'

'Yessir.'

'And are there always two women?'

'Yessir.'

'Have you ever seen any passengers aboard the ship?'

'Never.'

Therefore, the women must not have been the main attraction, but an accessory – an option, like they say when you're buying a car.

But then what were they doing aboard the *Halcyon*?

*

That evening, as he was driving home to Marinella, he remembered that there was no dinner waiting for him at home, as Adelina was still ill.

Ingrid was waiting for him at the door. She'd come in a grey car that looked like a torpedo.

'Sorry, but we're going to have to go out to eat.'

'Shall we go to the place that serves all those delicious antipasti?'

'All right. Get in.'

'I wouldn't dream of it. You get in.'

'I refuse to ride in that torpedo.'

'Come on, have a little faith.'

He got out, sat down in Ingrid's car, put on his seat belt, and the car took off. Montalbano closed his eyes, then opened them again at the sound of screeching tyres.

'We're here!' said Ingrid.

'Just give me a few minutes to recover,' said the inspector.

SIX

They stuffed themselves with so many antipasti that they were barely able to swallow the sea bass they'd ordered for the main course. As a result, when they were finished, they had trouble getting up from the table, even though they'd helped themselves to a couple of *digestivi*.

'Shall we go to my place to talk?' Montalbano asked in the end, somewhat reluctantly.

'Got any whisky?'

'As much as you like.'

'Let's go!'

*

Montalbano had the distinct impression that from the time he opened the door to get in her car to the moment he opened it to get out, not more than five seconds had passed.

How had Ingrid managed to take even less time than on the outward journey?

They sat outside on the veranda, with the whisky bottle and a couple of glasses within reach.

It was an evening so friendly to life that the light breeze seemed there to rock one to sleep.

And the lapping of the surf was like a lullaby.

Montalbano didn't feel much like launching into a question-and-answer session. He wished he could just sit there until his eyelids drooped.

It was Ingrid who took the initiative. And she did so with finesse.

'I have to get up very early tomorrow,' she said. 'I have to catch a plane at eight.'

'Where are you off to?'

'Paris. I'm going with a girlfriend who bought herself a flat in the Latin Quarter. I'll be away for a week.'

Which meant: Dear Salvo, please hurry up and ask me what you have to ask me. With Ingrid there was no need to beat around the bush or to mince one's words.

'Do you know a certain Giovanni Trincanato?'

'Of course.'

'Do you know him well?'

Ingrid smiled.

'Are you asking if I've slept with him?'

'I merely asked you if you knew him well. You're perfectly aware that I'm not interested in those kinds of details.'

'I couldn't say I know him well, but I know a lot about him.'

'Did you know he's in trouble?'

Ingrid giggled.

'Giogiò in trouble? I don't believe it.'

The fact that he went by the name Giogiò increased the inspector's antipathy for him.

'You haven't heard the news that he was forced to shut down the business?'

'Yes, that I knew.'

'And so? Why do you say you don't believe that he's in trouble?'

'Come on, Salvo! The fact that his business has been shut down doesn't mean that Giogiò is in trouble personally!'

'I get it,' said the inspector. 'So you're imagining that, even if he had to shut things down, he's not going to lose a cent?'

'Giogiò is one of the most unscrupulous men I've ever met,' said Ingrid. 'I have to say that sometimes it is that very fact that makes him seem fascinating to me.'

'Give me an example.'

'Well, I'll give you just one, but I think it'll be enough. His father didn't want to leave him the reins of his company; he knew him too well, and knew that Giogiò was liable to squander it all at the gaming table.'

'Or between the sheets.'

'That, too. At any rate, his father's idea was to create a sort of oversight committee for the company; Giogiò would be practically excluded from management while nominally remaining the head. Most importantly, he was not going to have any access to the money, aside from his monthly stipend. But not a euro more.'

'Who told you these things?'

'He told me himself, one evening when he'd hit the bottle. When Giogiò drinks, he gets a little loose-lipped. I would never tell him any secrets of my own. After a couple of glasses, the whole town would know.'

'OK, go on.'

'Well, when his father decided to draw up a will, he asked Giogiò to call the lawyer, since he could no longer get out of bed. In the presence of his father Giogiò took out his mobile and rang the lawyer, who replied that he was leaving to visit his brother in the United States, but that in case of an emergency he would send a replacement. The old man, who sensed that he didn't have much time left, said that was all right. Two days later the replacement arrived and took down the father's last will. And Giogiò's dad died that same evening.'

'So how is it that—'

'Come on, Salvo! Don't you get it? You, of all people, the brilliant Inspector Montalbano?'

'I'm sorry, but . . .'

'That phone call over his mobile was fake, Salvo. Giogiò never spoke to the lawyer. He made up that story about the guy's imminent departure for the US right there on the spot. And the replacement who drafted the will was an accomplice, a lawyer friend of Giogiò's.'

As an example of unscrupulousness, it was perfect. The stuff of textbooks and manuals.

'Do you know what Trincanato's relationship with the *Halcyon* is?'

'What's the *Halcyon*?'

Montalbano explained. Ingrid didn't know anything about the affair, and she was clearly being sincere.

'If you want, I can call you when I get back, and if you're still interested I can try to inform myself.'

'Thanks.'

'Come on, give me a little more whisky, and then I'll go.'

*

'You know what, Chief?'

'If you tell me, then I'll know.'

'Last night, some people unknown broke into Trincanato's garage.'

'And what did they do?'

'They torched the three cars that were in there.'

'Three cars?'

'Yes, sir: a Mercedes, a Ferrari, and a Fiat Panda. The Montelusa fire department had to put out the blaze.'

'Did you go and have a look?'

'No.'

'How about Augello?'

'No.'

So the police didn't intervene?

'Why not?'

'Because Trincanato reported the incident to the carabinieri.'

'So much the better,' commented the inspector. Then, still looking at Fazio: 'Were you expecting something like this?'

'Yeah. But I was thinking they'd do something to the factory instead.'

'Not me. Not the factory. Workers aren't likely to damage their workplace.'

*

After eight straight days of dead calm, the inspector could no longer stand the pointless shuffling between home and office.

He was beginning to lose his mind always doing nothing – or worse, always signing papers.

Finally, by the grace of God, on the ninth day, as he was going to bed feeling disconsolate, he received the call from Livia he'd so long been waiting for.

'We're returning to Genoa tomorrow.'

'Well, that's certainly good news.'

'What do you plan on doing?'

'If you want, I'll come.'

'Of course I want you to come.'

'Then I'll take the morning flight tomorrow . . .'

'Better not tomorrow morning.'

'Why not?'

'Salvo, try and understand. I've been away from home for a long time. Who knows what kind of condition I'll find it in. I want to put the place back in order and I also—'

'OK, I get it. So I'll come the day after tomorrow.'

'I'll be waiting for you.'

He had to hang on for just a little longer.

*

As soon as he got to the office the following morning, he rang Athos Fornaciari.

'Montalbano, I do hope you aren't going to ask for a further deferral!'

God, this guy was unpleasant.

'I've never been heard not to keep my word.' Nice to get that little rhyme in there.

'And so?'

'And so you can consider me on leave as of tomorrow.'

One hour later, Augello came in and informed him that Hizzoner the C'mishner had called and put him in charge of the station in the inspector's absence.

'See? I was right!' said Montalbano.

And so when he left for Boccadasse, his mind was at rest.

*

The plane took off an hour late, but nobody deigned to give any hint of the whys or wherefores. This is how airline and railway passengers are treated these days; and should any passenger venture to ask for an explanation he risks getting thrown out of the window.

So by the time he opened the door to Livia's apartment, it was almost noon.

Livia had told him she had to go to the office and therefore wouldn't be home. But he wanted to ring her just to let her know he'd arrived.

Another woman answered the phone.

'Montalbano here. I'm looking for Livia Burlando.'

'She's not at her desk. Please hold and I'll go and look for her.'

The music that came on the line was a familiar piece, Ravel's *Bolero,* perhaps chosen expressly to prepare the listener for a long wait. Which in fact turned out to be short. 'Director's secretary here. To whom am I speaking?' asked a chilly female voice.

What was this, some kind of ministry?

'Montalbano's the name. I was looking for Miss Livia Burlando.'

The woman's voice immediately became more human. 'Hello, Inspector. I'm Annamaria. Livia's in a meeting with the director preparing a report of their recent trip. If you want, I can try to—'

'No, please don't bother. Just tell her to give me a call when you see her.'

He opened his suitcase, put his stuff in the wardrobe, then went and found a chair, took it out onto the balcony, sat down, and started gazing at the sea.

A dress rehearsal for retirement?

When Livia called, it was already past one o'clock.

'Unfortunately I can't make it home for lunch. I'll be back around six. But everything's all ready for you in the oven. I prepared it this morning before leaving for work. All you need to do is heat it up.'

Montalbano felt a cold shiver run down his spine. This was truly bad news.

'Well, if you don't mind, I'd rather go to a restaurant.'

'No, come on. We can go this evening.'

Livia in the kitchen was a real disaster. Better a bout of quartan fever, a blown-out knee, or delirium tremens than to eat a meal prepared by her.

Indeed, from the very first bite he realized that the pasta was overcooked and the sauce tasted acidic. He contented himself with the mullet in tomato, which would have been marginally edible after a month of total fasting. He threw the pasta into the toilet and flushed. Then he got rid of the taste in his mouth by brewing a coffee so *ristretto* that it condensed into about twenty drops. But it was exactly what was needed.

He went and lay down for what he decided would be an hour's nap. But in the end it was Livia who woke him.

*

It was eight o'clock when he got up.

'Where should we go out to eat?' Livia asked him.

'Wherever you like.'

'Let's go to the Porto Antico; there's a restaurant there which . . . I went there with Eugenio before leaving.'

'And who's Eugenio?'

'Eugenio Barenghi, my boss.'

'So you're that familiar with him?'

'We've known each other practically our whole lives!'

*

There was no question that one ate quite well in that restaurant. The problem, however, was that Montalbano no longer had any appetite.

Because he'd suddenly remembered two things.

The first one was that Livia had told him that there were three of them going on that business trip: her, the director, and his secretary, Annamaria.

The second was that Annamaria, the secretary, had said quite specifically over the phone: '. . . preparing a report of their recent trip.'

Their recent trip. Not *our* recent trip.

Which meant that she had not gone away with Livia and dear old Eugenio. Livia, therefore, had lied to him.

'What's wrong?'

'Nothing.'

'That's not true. You're suddenly in a bad mood. You haven't even asked me how my trip went!'

'How did your trip go?'

He'd parroted her phrase on purpose, to show that he wasn't interested. Now it was Livia who got angry.

'It went great! Also because I wasn't with people who pull a long face just—'

'People? How many of you were there? A caravan?'

'No. There were . . . three of us.'

Her slight hesitation was not lost on the inspector.

Who darkened even further.

How should he act? Should he expose her lie? That would surely send the whole evening down the tubes . . .

How was it possible that their first day together should end in a spat? Wasn't it better to put the argument off until tomorrow? There would certainly be plenty of time for it, after all.

Anyway, Livia certainly didn't seem to have changed at all. On the contrary. She'd made love with great gusto, with sincere joy at seeing him again . . .

So why was he immediately imagining the worst? Why did he have such a nasty disposition, always picking holes in things?

'I'm sorry.'

'I'll wait for you outside,' said Livia, since the waiter was taking forever to bring them the bill.

Five minutes later, Montalbano paid, put the mobile that Livia had forgotten into his pocket, went outside himself, and looked around for her. He finally spotted her about ten yards away and called to her.

But as he was walking towards her, his path was cut off by a young woman. He had to stop to avoid running into her, and the girl did the same.

They looked at each other. It was Carmencita. 'Boss!' she cried.

And she threw her arms around his neck and kissed him on the cheek. She seemed truly happy to see him again.

She was wearing a different miniskirt this time, though it was just as short as the one she'd had on the only other time he'd seen her.

Montalbano was flummoxed. He'd imagined she was still aboard the *Halcyon*. The fifteen days didn't seem up yet. Out of the corner of his eye he saw Livia turn her back on him and start walking quickly towards the spot where she'd parked the car.

He could have just left Carmencita in the lurch and run after Livia, but he didn't want to waste the opportunity.

'Good evening,' said the girl, smiling at him.

'Good evening,' he replied. 'What are you doing here?'

'*Yo . . . espero un amigo . . . vamos al restaurante.*'

The inspector suddenly had an idea.

'*Yo deseo hablar con ti,*' he said, hoping his Spanish was comprehensible.

'*¿Ahora?*' the girl asked doubtfully.

'*No ahora . . . Mañana por la mañana . . .*'

He extracted Livia's mobile from his pocket and showed it to her.

'*¿Tu número?*'

The girl took the mobile out of his hand, keyed in her number, and gave it back to him.

At that moment a burly young man of about thirty appeared and, without saying a word, took Carmencita by one arm and dragged her away. She turned around.

'Good evening!' she repeated to him.

Montalbano stood there watching the two until they entered the restaurant. There was something about that man . . . he had the impression he'd seen him somewhere before. But where? He couldn't remember.

Then he wrote Carmencita's number on a piece of paper and deleted it from Livia's mobile.

Then, instinctively, and almost without realizing, he turned around and went back into the restaurant. He stopped and looked around the room. Carmencita and her friend were sitting at the table where he and Livia had been earlier.

The girl had her back to him and was speaking to the young man. A waiter came up to the inspector.

'Are you waiting to be seated?'

'No, I think I left my fountain pen here.'

'Where were you sitting?'

Montalbano pointed towards Carmencita's table. The waiter went over, looked around, asked the man something, who shook his head no and looked over at Montalbano.

The inspector then remembered who he was.

Giogiò's bodyguard. He'd seen him in Trincanato's waiting room on the day of the slap.

'I'm sorry, but they couldn't find anything,' said the waiter.

'No problem,' said Montalbano.

When he arrived at the parking spot, there was neither hide nor hair of Livia's car.

So he started looking for a taxi, thinking he was in for a long night.

SEVEN

Since he hadn't brought his own set of keys with him, he had to ring the buzzer. Out of pure and simple spite, Livia made him wait a long time before buzzing him in. And when he reached her landing, the door to her apartment was locked. So he had to buzz again.

He waited forever. Clearly Livia's intention was to make him pay, with her thumb on the scale, for his chance encounter with Carmencita.

And when Livia came and opened the door in her dressing gown, she looked as if she had just woken up. Opening the door a hair-thin crack, she went back into the bedroom without saying a word.

Montalbano went into the bathroom, got undressed, washed, and decided to go to bed himself. He didn't feel much like watching TV.

It was very dark in the bedroom, but he was absolutely certain that Livia was not asleep. No doubt she was crouching like a panther in the depths of the forest, ready to pounce.

Taking advantage of the faint light filtering in from outside, he reached his side of the bed, raised the light covers, and lay down.

Five minutes of total silence went by. Then the panther emerged from her den.

'I thought you were going to spend the night with that little slut,' Livia said suddenly. 'So what happened? Did she change her mind at the last minute? Find a better customer?'

'Don't talk crap. You're talking like a little bitch.'

'Well, I may talk like a bitch, but you act like an arsehole!'

Montalbano sat up in bed and turned on the light on his side. If there was to be a battle, they should at least be able to look each other in the eye.

'Tell me how I acted like an arsehole.'

Before answering, Livia likewise turned on the light on her side of the bed.

Goodbye, sleep! thought Montalbano.

'How you acted?!'

'Yes, how did I act?'

'Hahaha! So with me, Mr Muckymuck is in a bad mood, plays stick-in-the-mud, I have to squeeze the words out of him, but the minute he runs into the little slut, he's all smiles! He melts like ice cream!'

'So I was smiling?'

'Yes, you were smiling! Positively beaming! And if you say now that you weren't aware of it, that's even worse!'

'Livia, try and listen for a minute. All I ever did was give that girl a lift in my car almost two weeks ago.'

The inspector was trying to clear things up, but by now Livia was on a roll.

'And she still remembers you? Two weeks later? How many lifts have you given her, anyway?'

'Don't be ridiculous!'

'Me, ridiculous? You're the ridiculous one: a sixty-year-old man who lets himself be hugged and kissed like that by a little girl!'

'Like *what*?! What was I supposed to do, shoot her?'

'Just keep her at a distance! You could be her grandfather!'

At the sound of the word 'grandfather', Montalbano saw red.

Up until that point he'd managed not to complicate matters, but that 'grandfather' made him snap.

'I'm telling you the absolute truth, while you have done nothing but lie to me!'

'Me?!'

'Yes, ma'am! You!'

'When?'

'This very evening, at the restaurant, when you said there were three of you who went on that trip – you, the secretary, and your dear Eugenio, whom you've known your whole life!'

'And you're saying that's not true?'

'Yes.'

'And I repeat that the three of us went on that trip!'

'You see what a liar you are? I, purely by chance, found out from Annamaria herself that she didn't go.'

'She told you herself?'

'Yes. When I called the office to talk to you, and you were with your Eugenio and couldn't be disturbed because—'

'You haven't understood a thing!'

'Don't insist; it just makes things worse.'

'I don't care. I repeat: she went on the trip with us, but after two days Eugenio decided it would be best if she went back.'

'Aha!'

'What's that supposed to mean? "Aha!"?'

'It means that your Eugenio, seeing how things were going – with a good strong wind in his sails, I imagine – decided that three's a crowd and that "it would be best", as you say, to get that third party out of there!'

'Stop being such an idiot! You're making a complete fool of yourself! It's pathetic! What happened was that—'

'Yes, talk, talk. Let's hear what you can make up next!'

'But why am I wasting my breath and losing sleep with you? Good night!' said Livia, enraged.

She turned off her light and rolled over, facing away from him.

'Good night,' said Montalbano, enraged.

And he turned away as well, after extinguishing his light.

*

They tossed and turned in bed for about an hour, then, little by little, fell asleep. And their two bodies – which knew each other well and had no reason whatsoever to quarrel, and indeed liked each other and over time had grown increasingly fond of each other – slowly came closer and closer until, at the first light of dawn, they were stuck together.

And it was also their two bodies that dispelled the bad feelings and rancorous words of the night before.

*

Montalbano had left his mobile at home in Marinella, and therefore had to stay in until ten thirty.

He didn't dare call any earlier. But there was no answer. In fact, there was nothing at all: no ring, no busy signal, no indication that her phone was turned off. It was as if he'd dialled a non-existent number.

And yet he was certain he'd copied the number correctly onto the piece of paper, because he'd checked it before deleting it from Livia's phone.

The only possible explanation was that Carmencita was still asleep. She was not the type to get much of her sleep at night.

Then he got lost in another thought: what were the girl and the bodyguard doing in Genoa?

Want to bet . . . ?

At once he phoned the Genoa police commissioner's office.

'Hello? Could I please speak to Vice-Commissioner Giampaoli?'

'Who's calling?'

'This is Montalbano.'

He had Giampaoli on the line at once. 'Salvo! Is that you?'

'Hello, Stefano.'

'I haven't heard from you for ages! How are you?'

'Fine, thanks. And you?'

'Where are you calling from?'

Uh-oh. If he said he was calling from Genoa, he would never manage to wriggle out of a dinner invitation. Aside from the fact that he didn't feel like seeing anyone, there was the aggravating circumstance that Giampaoli was a vegetarian and the inspector really didn't feel like dining on meat or fish in front of someone like that. It made him feel like a bloodthirsty executioner.

'From Vigàta. I need a little favour.'

'Let's hear it.'

'I'd like to know whether a sailing ship called at the marina—'

'What marina?'

Montalbano hesitated.

'Don't tell me there's no marina in Genoa!'

'I'm not. I'm asking you which one.'

He wasn't at all sure; it was only a conjecture, really. Better keep things vague. 'I don't know.'

He heard Giampaoli muttering to himself.

'Is that a problem?' he asked.

'No, just a waste of time,' said Giampaoli. 'Go on.'

'I want to know if there's a big schooner flying the Bolivian flag. It's called the *Halcyon* . . .'

'I'll try to do what I can. But you have to understand, it won't be easy. Are you sure it's actually in Genoa proper?'

'What do you mean?'

'Come on, Salvo. The city is surrounded by marinas. Have you forgotten what the Riviera is like? There are marinas galore!'

'Well, see what you can do. I'll call you back around five this evening.'

*

He went out to eat at a restaurant just a few steps from Livia's front door, with windows open to the sea and a small beach beside it.

Montalbano enjoyed himself immensely. The place smelled like home.

Before going to the beach for a stroll, he went back to Livia's apartment to ring Carmencita again.

This time, too, there was no answer.

*

He slept until half-past four, and at five he called Giampaoli.

'Salvo, you are one lucky bastard.'

'Tell me everything.'

'Your *Halcyon* put in at Varazze the evening of the day before yesterday, but it put out again yesterday morning, headed for Malta. It dropped off its only two female passengers . . . If you want, I can give you their names.'

'Let's have them.'

'Joan Crowling, American, and Carmen Lopez, Spanish.'

It all made sense now.

'Did any other people board?'

'No. It left with just the crew.'

The *Halcyon* was therefore in the habit of staying in a port for the absolute minimum amount of time necessary and then disappearing.

So where did the other passengers disembark?

And how could Carmencita be in the company of Trincanato's bodyguard if he didn't also arrive with the schooner?

Maybe they'd planned to meet in Genoa?

He tried Carmencita's number again, but the result was the same as before. And he suddenly understood the reason for her silence.

Just as he had recognized the bodyguard, so the bodyguard had recognized him. A police inspector.

And he'd forbidden Carmencita to answer. Her mobile was probably at the bottom of the sea by now.

Then he had an idea that seemed interesting to him. He wrote a note for Livia:

If I'm not at home when you get back, wait for me. I won't be long.

And he called a taxi.

'Where do you want to go?'

'To Cristoforo Colombo.'

The taxi driver, instead of driving off, turned around and looked at him.

'What is it?' asked Montalbano.

'Sir, everything around here is called Cristoforo Colombo. Streets, hotels, restaurants . . .'

'I want to go to the airport.'

He didn't know anyone at the airport police commissariat. He introduced himself, giving his profession and rank, and they were very polite.

Half an hour later he was on his way back to Boccadasse, convinced that the bodyguard had come to Genoa to wait for the *Halcyon*'s arrival and collect the two girls.

Apparently they didn't want them to have any contact with anyone.

And the bodyguard, like a good dog, had accompanied Joan to the airport and stayed by Carmencita's side until her likely departure. By now he was probably back in Vigàta.

*

'Shall we stay at home and cook something?'

Heaven forbid! The danger had to be averted.

'I'd rather go out. In Vigàta I'm always dining at home and alone, and—'

'Am I supposed to believe that?'

'Believe what?'

'That you always dine alone?'

'You want to start that up again?'

'I was just kidding. And just to show my good faith, I can tell you I saw the little slut again.'

Montalbano gave a start. 'You saw Carmencita?'

'What a cliché of a name! Yes, I saw her.'

'Are you sure it was her?'

'Absolutely certain. And you may not be so pleased to learn that she was in the company of a massive young man who was holding her tight.'

'Where were they?'

'They were coming out of a hotel.'

Montalbano made a decision.

And he told her everything, in full detail, from the time Joan the American came to the station to report a purse-snatching to the lift he gave Carmencita, to Trincanato's mysterious relationship with the *Halcyon*, to the call he made to Giampaoli, and, finally, to his visit to the airport police station.

'And now you have to help me.'

Livia gave him a confused look. 'Me? How?'

'Before we go to the restaurant, let's pass by that hotel. I'll keep out of sight, but I want you to get out of the car and see if the receptionist can tell you how long Miss Lopez will be staying.'

'Then what?'

'Then, if she's going to be here for all of tomorrow, we'll work out a way for me to get in touch with her, even if only for a few moments, without the bodyguard knowing.'

He was expecting Livia to make a fuss, but in reality she seemed thrilled with the idea of playing policewoman.

'Let me get dressed, and then we can go.'

*

Montalbano remained seated in the car, waiting for Livia to return. He didn't want to be seen anywhere near the hotel. If he ran into the bodyguard, the whole plan would go to the dogs.

Some twenty minutes later, he saw Livia coming towards the car. He opened the door for her.

'And so?'

Livia seemed satisfied.

'You know what? I pretended I was a Spanish woman who spoke good Italian. I told the receptionist I was a cousin of Carmencita Lopez, and he said she'd gone out. She and the bodyguard don't sleep together; they have separate rooms. The receptionist told me that Mr Fantuzzo – that's the guy's name – had called from the hotel to reserve a seat for Carmencita Lopez on a flight for Barcelona tomorrow. She'll be leaving the hotel at noon. Did I do a good job?'

'You did a great job!'

So he'd been wrong to think the two had already left Genoa.

'But I still can't work out why Joan left almost immediately after she got here, whereas Carmencita stayed behind,' Montalbano said as they drove to the restaurant.

'There are two plausible answers to that question,' replied Livia. 'The first is that Carmencita and Fantuzzo decided to take a brief holiday together. The second is that Carmencita had an appointment in Genoa with a client she met on board the *Halcyon*. And Fantuzzo had to stay to keep an eye on her.'

'It's also possible that Carmencita decided to spend her free time away from her client with Fantuzzo,' the inspector added.

'Sure, why not? Mixing business with pleasure,' Livia commented, using a cliché that got a little under Montalbano's skin.

They arrived at the restaurant and sat down. 'What do you think you'll do?'

'It's a difficult situation. We'll have to seize the moment when Fantuzzo leaves her alone. Because by now it's clear that he never lets her out of his sight, and that it was he who told her not to answer her phone.'

'But do you have any ideas?'

'The only thing I can do is go and set myself up outside the hotel tomorrow morning – starting, say, around nine. If I see Fantuzzo come out, I rush in and lay my cards out on the table. I tell them I'm a police inspector and have to speak to Carmencita. I merely need enough time to ask her one question. If, on the other hand, I see them come out of the hotel together on their way to the airport, I'll follow them in a taxi and, once there, try somehow to distract Fantuzzo, maybe by seeking help from my colleagues in the airport police force.'

'Will you promise me one thing?' asked Livia.

'Sure.'

'Will you keep me informed? Just give me a ring. I won't be able to hold out until six p.m. without knowing how it all turned out.'

'OK, I promise.'

The waiter came to their table to take their order. And from that moment on, Montalbano and Livia spoke no more about the subject.

*

Livia left the house at seven-thirty the next morning to go to the office. Montalbano took things more slowly and arrived outside the hotel at nine o'clock sharp.

Seeing a kiosk nearby, he bought four newspapers and set himself up at a table in a cafe just opposite the hotel.

It only appeared to be an ideal lookout post.

The problem was that there was a great deal of traffic of bodies in and around the hotel. Mobs of tourists kept arriving, and just as many kept leaving without interruption. At least, from his position, the big tourist buses didn't block his view. At any rate, he couldn't afford to distract himself for even a moment by reading the paper.

EIGHT

More than two hours later, he'd downed four coffees and a lemon soda to loosen his pasty tongue, and still not a trace of Fantuzzo. Maybe he had felt no need to leave the hotel before departure.

Because he would definitely be accompanying Carmencita to the airport.

The inspector couldn't bear staying shut up in that cafe for another second.

By now it would have been clear even to a blind man that he was sitting there just to watch the entrance to the hotel.

And there was also a waiter who every so often looked over at him with a mocking smile. He'd probably taken him for a cuckolded husband trying to catch his unfaithful wife in flagrante.

He paid and left.

He stopped in front of a shop window that reflected the hotel entrance. After five minutes of pretending to look inside, his eyes finally focused on what was displayed:

intimate feminine apparel. He stepped away at once, worried they might take him for a sex maniac.

Another five minutes gained by looking into another display window, belonging to a shoe shop. To keep an eye on the movements outside the hotel, however, he had to twist his neck.

Luckily an African man approached, selling socks so colourful that it practically hurt one's eyes just to look at them. Montalbano immediately took advantage of the opportunity and spent ten minutes selecting a pair of embarrassingly green and red socks, then wasted a little more time bargaining over the price.

Then he looked at his watch. It was noon, the hour at which Carmencita was supposed to leave the hotel.

He lingered another five minutes and then went in.

He decided not to identify himself. Half of Japan seemed to have gathered around the front desk. He waited his turn, never taking his eyes off the stairs and lift.

'May I help you?'

'Yes. Miss Carmen Lopez, please.'

'Miss Lopez has already left.'

He hesitated. 'When?'

'She left the hotel at eight o'clock this morning.'

He just stood there, stunned and slack-jawed, not knowing what to think.

The receptionist gave him a questioning look. Meanwhile, an entire prairie of Texans – tall, blond, and wearing cowboy boots and hats – was forming behind the inspector.

As soon as he recovered, Montalbano managed to ask: 'Mr Fantuzzo, too?'

'Yes, him, too.'

He cut a swathe through the cowboys, ran outside, and took the first free taxi.

'The airport, please.'

*

At the airport police station, they were slightly – but only slightly – less polite than the first time.

They spent some ten minutes, if that, explaining to him how Miss Lopez had indeed reserved for the two p.m. flight to Barcelona but then showed up at eight-thirty that morning and managed to get her ticket changed for the eleven o'clock flight.

Mr Ernesto Fantuzzo, for his part, had left for Punta Raisi Airport in Palermo on the eleven-fifteen flight.

Happy? Let's say yes.

'Next time, Montalbano, there's no need to come all the way out here. By now we know you. All you have to do is call,' said his colleague, saluting him.

Was the man making fun of him? The inspector was almost sure of it, based on the grin on his face.

Before getting into a taxi back to town, he rang Livia and told her what had happened.

'So, in conclusion, they really, brilliantly fu—'

'No obscenities!'

'. . . screwed us!'

'But how could they have known that—'

'Maybe the receptionist told Carmencita that a cousin of hers had asked for her. And since either Carmencita has no female cousins, or, if she does, they're in Spain, or, if they're here in Genoa, they never come calling, Fantuzzo no doubt became suspicious. And covered their tracks.'

'So, what do we do now?'

'What do you think? We do nothing.'

*

He was hanging around in the flat when around half-past four he suddenly felt like phoning Fazio to find out whether there was any news.

The voice of the switchboard operator was not Catarella's.

'Who are you?'

'Who are *you*, rather!'

'Montalbano.'

'The inspector?'

'Until proven otherwise.'

'I'm terribly sorry, sir, but I'm new here.'

'What's your name?'

'Pappalardo.'

Never heard of him.

'Where did you come from?'

'From Montelusa Central.'

'Is Catarella unwell?'

'No, sir.'

It didn't make sense.

'Get me Fazio, would you?'

'He's not in.'

'How about Inspector Augello?'

'Inspector Augello is no longer employed at this commissariat.'

'He's no longer employed there?'

'No, sir.'

'So where is he?'

'At Montelusa Central.'

It felt like a dream. He couldn't believe what he'd just heard.

What the hell was this? An earthquake?

'Is Catarella still working there?'

'Yes, sir.'

'Where is he?'

'With the motorized unit.'

'Why is he not at the switchboard?'

'Those were Inspector Stracquadanio's instructions.'

'And who is Inspector Stracquadanio?'

'The interim chief.'

'Since when?'

'Since the day before yesterday.'

Montalbano had a flash. Want to bet Hizzoner the C'mishner took advantage of his absence to launch a blitz? The giant fucking arsehole! First, he reassures him and Augello, and then . . .

'Get me Catarella.'

'Straightaway, sir.'

'Whoozziss?'

He sounded like a castaway in an unknown land. 'It's Montalbano, Cat.'

'Ah, Chief, Chief! Ah, Chief, Chief!'

'Listen, Cat . . .'

'Ah, Chief ,Chief!'

Catarella was weeping disconsolately. The inspector would never be able to find out what happened from him.

'Listen, Cat, try to find a way to tell Fazio that I'll be waiting for a phone call from him at Livia's place, as of this moment. Understand?'

'Poifickly. Ah, Chief, Chief!'

Ten minutes later Fazio's call came in.

'Would you please tell me what the fuck—'

'Well, the very day you left, the commissioner called Inspector Augello and told him that, contrary to what had been originally decided, he would have to leave the Vigàta station and immediately start working at Montelusa Central in the passport office, and his place would be taken by Inspector Virginio Stracquadanio, for the express purpose of reorganizing the Vigàta commissariat.'

'Reorganizing?'

'Yes, sir. That's the exact word he used.'

'And so all this reorganization consists of grabbing poor Catarella and moving him to the motorized unit?'

'Not only.'

'Meaning?'

'In addition to Augello, I also am supposed to start working in Montelusa from next week.'

Bonetti-Alderighi's plan suddenly became clear. To dismantle the Vigàta commissariat.

It was equally clear that Hizzoner the C'mishner had

himself got the personnel office to cook up the whole unused leave business, forcing the inspector to go on holiday.

'Ah, Chief, I wanted to mention that a letter arrived for you today, from the personnel office,' said Fazio.

'Who's got it now?'

'I do. I told them to have all mail addressed to you delivered to me. I didn't want this Stracquadanio to confuse personal mail and official mail.'

'Well done. Could you read the letter to me?'

'I'll call you back in ten minutes.'

Montalbano essentially spent the next ten minutes cursing the saints.

Then Fazio called back and read him the letter, which was signed by Athos Fornaciari.

It said that after a careful review of the situation, it turned out that the computation of unused leave days had been erroneous, and that the unused time added up to double the figure originally arrived at. And, *consequently*, as a preliminary measure, Inspector Salvo Montalbano was required to absent himself from his duties not for ten (10) days, as previously indicated, but indeed for thirty (30).

If he had any doubts before, they were now entirely dispelled.

It was a veritable conspiracy, organized with dastardly intelligence.

To make him a stranger in his own police department. To put him in a position where he no longer had any friends or people he could trust, since by now he was too old and weary to start all over again.

That way, in the end they wouldn't even have to ask him to resign; he himself would file for retirement out of sheer exhaustion, estrangement, and incompatibility.

He made another snap decision.

'Listen, I'm coming back tomorrow. But you mustn't tell anyone. And I want you to come to my place in the evening.'

Then he immediately called Adelina, informed her that he was returning, and asked her kindly to refill the fridge. His plan was to eat lunch and dinner at home for three days, without letting anyone know he was back in town.

*

When Livia came home, she took one look at his face and asked: 'What happened?'

'Why do you ask?'

'I can see something's wrong. I know you too well.'

Montalbano cracked and told her everything. By the time he had finished, his hands were trembling with rage.

'I agree that it's a good idea for you to go back and see with your own eyes what's really happening. But what do you think you'll do?'

'To be honest, I haven't got the slightest idea.'

'I have just one piece of advice. They'll probably try to provoke you, to trick you into making a false move. Be very careful.'

'I would feel more reassured if you were with me.'

Livia remained silent for a few moments, then said:

'Call me every evening and keep me abreast of the situation and how it develops. I can probably come down briefly, not this weekend, but the one after.'

*

When he got to the airport and tried to buy a ticket, they told him the flight was full. If he wanted, he could take the next flight, which left at eight that evening. Which meant that he would get home at night and miss his appointment with Fazio. A wasted day. On the other hand, spending the whole day at Genoa Airport was out of the question.

As he was heading towards the taxi stand, he heard someone call him.

'Montalbano!'

It was his colleague from the airport police.

'Why didn't you come and see us today?'

Was the guy mocking him?

Playing it cool, Montalbano explained that he'd been unable to leave because there were no seats available.

'Do you need to go to Palermo?'

'Yes.'

'Wait a second.' And he took out his phone and started talking. Then he said: 'I found you a place. Hurry. For once I was able to be useful to you.'

*

For the entire duration of his journey from Genoa to Palermo, and in the car from Palermo to Marinella, he did nothing but rack his brains over how to undo the damage being done to him by Bonetti-Alderighi.

He couldn't come up with a solution, but did not lose heart.

Adelina had made him a lot to eat, but his stomach felt tight and he wasn't very hungry.

He called Livia to tell her he'd arrived home safely, then he turned on the television, to see if there were any new developments. He tuned in just in time to hear the editorial commentary of Pippo Ragonese on TeleVigàta.

> *We have learned from a reliable source that, at the behest of the Montelusa police commissioner, Dr Bonetti-Alderighi, a radical renewal of the Vigàta Police Commissariat is currently under way. We cannot help but be delighted at such news. Here at TeleVigàta we have long been very critical of certain 'borderline' behaviours of Inspector Salvo Montalbano, who has been the head of that commissariat for many, indeed too many, years. A return to order should be beneficial. Inspector Montalbano is presently on compulsory leave, but rumours are circulating that he may soon be retiring. Many of his most loyal collaborators have already been transferred, or will be soon. We, I repeat, can only applaud . . .*

He turned it off. More than angry, he felt bewildered. There was something fishy in Ragonese's words.

Clearly the newsman had been tipped off by either the commissioner or someone close to him.

In short, Bonetti-Alderighi had wanted everyone to know what he had in mind. This, therefore, was not a conspiracy, as the inspector had thought, since conspiracies are carried out in darkness, on the sly, in silence . . .

And so?

He phoned the Free Channel. The secretary answered.

'Montalbano here. Is Nicolò in?'

'Inspector, how nice to hear from you! It's been so long! Hold on, I'll put him on at once.'

'Hello, Salvo. Where are you calling from?'

Better not tell him he was back.

'From Livia's in Boccadasse. Listen, have you heard anything about what's been going on at the station?'

'Of course. They dredged up some excuse to summon ten journalists, then, after a bit of nonsense, Dr Lattes began talking, as though incidentally, about your commissariat. First he said that it was a perfectly normal rotation of personnel, then a little later he used the expression "to clear the air". The general impression is that they want to screw you.'

'Listen, Nicolò, would you be willing to interview me?'

'Gladly, but I don't think I can come all the way to Boccadasse . . .'

'No, in that case I would take a plane down and come to you.'

'Then there's no problem.'

'Can I get some kind of advance?'

'Some what?'

'Could you give some advance notice of the interview? Could you announce it on today's evening news edition? But you have to say you'll be interviewing me in Boccadasse.'

'OK.'

Having made his intentions to 'reorganize' the Vigàta commissariat, clearly Bonetti-Alderighi was waiting for a reaction from the inspector. He would get it from the interview with Zito. The commissioner had made the first move; the second move was up to him.

Then he went and lay down.

*

He slept for three hours straight. And when he woke up he felt refreshed, lucid, and, most importantly, not at all agitated.

He'd been right to come back to Vigàta. Here he could fight on familiar ground.

His new-found calm stirred up a wolflike appetite. But it was still too early for dinner.

He got dressed, went down to the beach, reached the water's edge, and started walking until he finally had to kneel down in the sand from exhaustion like an overtaxed horse. It took him twice as long to walk home as it did to get to that point.

When he returned, he raced to open the oven and found a dish of *pasta 'ncasciata* inside. Licking his lips, he lit the oven to warm it up.

At half-past eight he turned on the television. Nicolò

Zito kept his word. At the end of the news report, he said that the following day he would broadcast an interview from Genoa with Inspector Montalbano.

At nine-thirty there was a knock at the door. He went and opened. It was Fazio.

They embraced.

NINE

But as soon as he sat Fazio down on the veranda and offered him a glass of wine, which he declined, the inspector practically attacked him.

'Would you please explain to me why neither you nor Augello felt the need to inform me of what was happening at the station?'

Fazio opened his mouth to answer, but Montalbano continued: 'I only found out by chance; if I hadn't wanted some news from home . . .'

He'd been carrying this question around with him since the previous day. It had kept him from sleeping. He'd taken Mimì's and Fazio's attitude as a kind of betrayal.

And since he hadn't been able to come up with any explanation whatsoever for that heavy silence, his nerves were presently about to snap like a spring stretched to its limit.

If they'd warned him in time, he might, by reacting at once, have been able to contain the damage.

'We talked about it, Chief . . . That's all we did, was

talk about whether we should call you or not. And in the end Inspector Augello said it was probably best if, for the time being, you didn't know what was going on.'

'And why did he think that?'

'Well, Augello maintains, and I agree with him, that we're dealing with a provocation on the part of the commissioner, who is trying to get you to make a false move, which would force you to resign. If you had found out what was happening right away, you might have made a rash decision and reacted the wrong way, making it easier for Bonetti-Alderighi to screw you.'

This made a certain sense.

Montalbano felt somewhat relieved. His men had not been remiss. On the contrary.

'All right, but now that I know, it's not like I can sit on the sidelines watching!'

Fazio paused before speaking.

'Sorry to say, Chief, but what's done is done.'

Montalbano felt confused. He couldn't believe that it was Fazio who'd said those words.

'So you're resigned to it?'

'It's not a question of being resigned or not.'

'Well, then, what is it?'

'If you'll allow me, Chief, I should tell you that I've given this whole thing a lot of thought.'

Montalbano pricked up his ears. Fazio was an excellent police officer and had a good, smart head on his shoulders. He'd never once heard him say anything off the wall just to hear the sound of his voice.

'And did you reach any conclusion?'

'Conclusion, no . . . However . . .'

'However?' Montalbano pressed him.

'There are a few things that don't make sense to me.'

'Such as?'

'I'll start with the first one. I'm convinced that if Bonetti-Alderighi really wanted to get you out of his hair, he would have come up with a better reason than your backlog of annual leave. For example, he could have arranged for an immediate transfer for you. And if you refused, he could have had you forcibly retired. With this business of the annual leave, on the other hand, a lot of time's going to pass before you get fed up and decide to go. Whereas the commissioner seems to be in a really big hurry.'

'Go on.'

'The second thing is this: why was Inspector Augello sent to Montelusa to work, and why will I have to do the same in a few days?'

'What are you getting at?'

Fazio started counting on his fingers.

'In Lampedusa they need personnel for all the migrant boat landings; the Fiacca commissariat still has no chief inspector and doesn't even have six units; same situation, more or less, in Campobello . . . So my question is: why didn't the commissioner send us to Lampedusa, Fiacca, or Campobello?'

Made perfect sense.

'What's your answer?' he asked Fazio.

'I'm under the impression he wants to keep us within reach, but away from the station. Bear in mind, too, that he could have arranged temporary, short-term transfers, but didn't . . .'

'And what could be the reason?'

'No idea.'

The phone rang.

'Excuse me,' said Montalbano, going and answering the phone in a falsetto. If it was the commissioner's office, he would say he was a distant cousin of the inspector's.

It was Nicolò Zito, who recognized his voice immediately.

'Would you please tell me why you've been bullshitting me?'

'Bullshitting you? How?'

'Telling me you were in Boccadasse, for example.'

'I apologize, Nicolò, but you see . . . Do you have any news?'

'Less than an hour after announcing our forthcoming interview, the commissioner's office called me.'

Montalbano turned on the speakerphone so that Fazio could hear, too.

'Who was it that called?'

'Dr Lattes.'

'What did he want?'

'He asked me if I knew where you were. Where I was going to do the interview. I told him we had yet to decide on the location, and that I was waiting for your phone call.'

'Well done.'

'Immediately afterwards, I tried to reach you in Boccadasse, but Livia told me you were here. I advised her that if anybody from the commissioner's office called, she should tell them she didn't know where you were. She was in the process of answering when the line went dead.'

'Nicolò, I want to kiss you.'

'There's one problem.'

'Let's hear it.'

'In my opinion, they don't want you to do this interview. They seem to have gone into panic mode the moment they heard about it.'

'I agree.'

'And since they can't put pressure on me, because I would start an uprising to defend the freedom of the press and so on, they'll try and pressure you.'

'I concur again. But I don't give a flying fuck.'

'Careful, though.'

'Why?'

'If tomorrow the commissioner was somehow to learn that you're in Marinella, he could send someone to get you and hold you at Montelusa Central all day under some pretext, and that would be the end of our interview.'

Good point.

'So what do you suggest?'

'That we do it sooner.'

'Meaning?'

'Come here to the Free Channel studios early tomorrow, at nine in the morning, and we'll do it right away.'

'All right.'

He hung up and looked over at Fazio. Who seemed doubtful.

'What's wrong?'

'I'm suspicious.'

'About what?'

'That phone call from Lattes to Zito.'

'What's suspicious about it?'

'Chief, have you forgotten that whenever you go on holiday, you're required to leave your location so you can be reached? Everyone in our department knew you were going to Boccadasse. Therefore the commissioner's office must also have known.'

The phone rang again.

'Let me answer,' said Fazio.

As soon as he heard who was on the other end, he said goodbye and passed the receiver to Montalbano.

'It's Livia,' he said.

Montalbano put the speakerphone back on. If Livia started talking about private matters, he would turn it off. 'Salvo, I tried phoning a little while ago, but the line was busy. I got a call from the Montelusa commissioner's office. They urgently needed to talk to you. I told them you were eating out. So they asked me to tell you to call Dr Lattes as soon as you got back. Then Nicolò called.'

'What time was it when you got the first call?'

'Nine o'clock. But there was also a third call.'

'Tell me about it.'

'The commissioner's office again. I told them you hadn't come home yet, and they rather emphatically told me you should call Lattes when you return, no matter what the hour of the night.'

'OK, thanks. We'll talk again tomorrow.' He hung up.

'What did I say, Chief?' said Fazio. 'First they called Boccadasse because they knew you were there; then, not finding you there, they asked themselves why you'd gone out to eat without Livia, they checked with Zito, and now they're convinced you're already back here.'

'So, like it or not, I now have no choice but to call Lattes,' the inspector concluded.

'But what are you going to tell him?'

'First I'll find out what he wants.'

He dialled Lattes's direct number.

'Montalbano here. You were looking for me?'

He distinctly heard the chief of the commissioner's cabinet sigh in relief.

'My dear inspector! What a pleasure to hear your voice! The family all doing well? The wife? The children?'

'All well.'

What a pain in the arse!

'Listen, my dear friend, the reason I'm disturbing you – for which I apologize – is that the commissioner learned that you were going to give an interview with the Free Channel, apparently concerning the ongoing reorganization of the Vigàta commissariat . . . Is that correct?'

'Yes.'

'*Ahem. Ahem.*'

'Do you have a cold?' Montalbano asked him, just to mess around.

Lattes seemed not to have heard.

'Well, let me begin by saying: please don't kill the messenger . . . I find myself in the unpleasant position of having to inform you that His Honour the Commissioner is completely against your giving any kind of interview. In fact, just to be clear, he formally enjoins you not to do it.'

'No, that can't be! What are you saying? I do hope you're joking!' said Montalbano, pretending to be scared to death.

'Unfortunately, no!'

'Oh, my God! I'm ruined! But look, I had no intention . . . Oh, my God, what a disaster!'

'Please let me finish. The commissioner says that if you go ahead and do the interview anyway, you should know that you will be facing harsh measures. He told me to tell you that, and now I've told you.'

'Damn! The horse!' exclaimed Montalbano.

Lattes, at the mention of a horse, which had nothing to do with anything, became flustered.

'Horse? What horse? What . . . are you talking about?'

'Damn damn damn!'

'Would you please tell me what you're talking about?' said Lattes.

'The horse has already left the stable! I've already done the interview! Why didn't you call me earlier?'

'Good Lord! When did you do that?'

Montalbano didn't answer right away. He was having

such a ball, he just kept on wailing in lament, as false as a three-euro note.

'But why didn't you try to reach me on my mobile?'

'We tried, but it was always turned off!'

'Oh, you're right . . . So I wouldn't be disturbed during the interview!'

'But when did you do it?' Lattes asked again.

'Just a few hours ago. I went out to dinner with the journalist that the Free Channel sent to get me, and immediately afterwards—'

'But then why did Mr Zito tell us you hadn't done it yet?'

'You called Zito?!' said Montalbano, dodging the question and pretending to be surprised and worried. 'I do hope you didn't order him not to broadcast the interview! You'll turn the entire press corps against you! That would be a terrible mistake!'

'No, I only . . . At any rate, Inspector, couldn't you just contact the journalist who interviewed you and ask him, in a friendly manner, not to broadcast it?'

'Look, Dr Lattes, I would gladly do that, but I haven't got his phone number. And since he's afraid to fly, he took the train. And at this moment he's in transit. I could address myself directly to Zito, but do you really think that's such a good idea, right after your imprudent call? He's a shrewd one, you know, and you can be sure he's already on the defensive. If you could suggest some other way, I would be quite happy to cooperate, believe me.'

'Listen to me carefully, Montalbano.'

'I'm all ears, Doctor.'

'Could you summarize for me – in a nutshell, of course – what you said in the interview?'

'Well, you see, being – certainly through no fault of my own – being, I repeat, through no fault of my own, completely in the dark as to His Honour the Commissioner's warning, I guess you could say I let myself go a little . . .'

'How far did you go?' Lattes asked, voice quavering.

'Well, the interview is, in effect, quite critical of what you call the "reorganization", which I define outright as an arbitrary, unjustified power grab. And I enumerate all the successes the Vigàta commissariat has had over the past decade, and I also announce that all the unions – indeed all – are mobilizing for—'

'Oh, sweet Jesus . . .' sighed Dr Lattes, by now on the verge of fainting. 'Did you say all the unions?'

'Yes, all.'

Lattes hung up without even saying goodbye.

'Are you really going to say all that tomorrow morning?' asked Fazio.

'Yes, except for the nonsense about the unions, which I made up on the spot to scare Lattes.'

They left it that they would be in touch by phone.

As soon as Fazio was gone, the inspector went to bed and slept deeply.

Now that the war with Bonetti-Alderighi was completely out in the open, he felt much better than the day before.

*

The following morning, as he was taking a shower, and then later, as he was consoling himself with a mugful of coffee, he reviewed everything he wanted to say in the interview.

He left the house at eight fifteen and drove off towards the Free Channel studios, which were on the outskirts of Montelusa.

As he was about to turn off the main road and into the large car park in front of the building, he saw, right outside the entrance, two cars of the Finance Police.

He stopped.

What on earth were the Finance Police doing at the Free Channel at that hour?

He remained undecided as to what to do. Going right in was not a good idea; it was better to wait a bit.

Then he saw Zito's secretary come out to smoke a cigarette.

He started the car back up, and when he reached the woman, he lowered the window. She recognized him and drew near.

'I came out on purpose, Inspector. I was waiting for you. Nicolò says it's better if you don't let anyone see you. The Finance Police are inside.'

'Thanks,' said the inspector, putting the car in gear.

*

Driving back to Marinella, he came to the conclusion that there was no way the Finance Police's inspection was a chance occurrence.

He had to tip his hat to Bonetti-Alderighi. In the chess game they were playing, the commissioner had made the right move.

Clearly the Finance Police could not confiscate the interview, which the commissioner thought had already been done. They probably wouldn't even mention it. In compensation they could drum up so many administrative problems that Nicolò wouldn't be able to broadcast any news for the entire day.

Now it was his turn. And that was the problem. What should he do? Which pawn should he move?

*

He came home to find Adelina bustling in the kitchen. He put an arm around her shoulders.

'What are you making for me?'

'Pasta witta clamma sauce an' mulless an' tamatas.' The aroma was already spellbinding.

The telephone rang.

'You answer, Adelì. I'll stand beside you and try to hear who it is.'

'Hello?'

'Is this the Montalbano home?'

'Yess'm.'

The inspector took the receiver out of her hand. 'Hello, Ingrid.'

'Hello, Salvo.'

'Who told you I—'

'I took a guess. I sensed that you wouldn't be able to

stay away from Marinella for very long. I'm calling because I want to tell you about something that happened to me last night.'

'I'm listening.'

'Wouldn't it be better if we met?'

'Whatever you prefer. This evening?'

'I can't this evening. Why don't you invite me to lunch?'

'OK. Come to Marinella. But be sure not to tell anyone I'm back. I mean it.'

He told Adelina to set the table for two and then went and sat in the armchair in front of the television, which he did not, however, turn on. He couldn't sit out on the veranda and enjoy the morning sun. He was afraid that someone might see him. For now it was better to remain hidden.

He started reflecting on what had happened.

TEN

There was something in the commissioner's move that made no sense whatsoever.

To prevent the Free Channel from airing the interview, which he thought had already been done, he'd sent the Finance Police. A branch of the military not under his jurisdiction. He must, therefore, have involved other authorities, the prefect, at the very least.

But how had he convinced them, if this was in fact the case? What excuse had he presented in order to win their cooperation? What sort of whopping lies had he dreamt up?

The 'reorganization' argument would have seemed ridiculous to the prefect and Finance Police. They would not have accepted it for an instant.

So what had he told them that could have seemed so critical as to persuade them to intervene?

And for what reason had Bonetti-Alderighi not used the full weight of his authority to shut the inspector down altogether and institute, once and for all, harsh disciplinary proceedings against him?

To put it bluntly, it was he, Montalbano, who was in the wrong. What the commissioner was doing with his station was well within his rights, even if the whole business was not at all to the inspector's liking. But *his* opinion didn't count; it carried no weight, and any contrary statement he might make could therefore be considered unwarranted and insubordinate. Some sort of official call to order was to be expected.

Except that Bonetti-Alderighi had not made a call to order, and seemed intent on never making one.

So the question was this: how far could he stretch the rubber band? How far could he go in provoking his superior?

Maybe it was best to sit tight for the moment and skip his turn, letting the commissioner make the next move, too.

It was possible he was starting to make a little sense of it all.

*

Ingrid didn't start talking until after they'd cleared the table.

'Do you remember that the last time we spoke, we said we were going to talk more about Giogiò?'

Montalbano hesitated. 'Who's Giogiò?'

'I'm sorry, Trincanato.'

The business of the commissioner's surprise attack had made him forget all about the story of the *Halcyon*.

What did it matter anymore, anyway? It seemed to

him like something out of the past. There were more serious problems to deal with.

'Ah yes, right,' he said, rather indifferently. Ingrid seemed miffed.

'Look, if you're not interested . . .'

'No, I am, I really am.'

'A mutual friend told me yesterday that Giogiò hasn't been seen around since yesterday evening. He's holed up in his house. They say he's scared out of his wits.'

'Well, he's already been sent one rather serious message: they torched his cars . . .'

'Yes, I know, but the car thing pissed him off, it didn't frighten him. Anyway, the culprits were arrested.'

Montalbano jumped out of his chair.

Why hadn't Fazio mentioned this? Apparently he'd forgotten.

'They were arrested?'

'Yes. By the carabinieri, while you were away.'

'Do you by any chance know who they were?'

'I was told that one of them was the son of a worker of Giogiò's who'd hanged himself.'

'So he's not scared about anything to do with the factory?'

'Apparently not.'

'And did your friend find out why he's so scared?'

'When she called him to find out how he was doing, Giogiò only gave her confused answers. He swore he'd stopped drinking, said he'd missed an opportunity he shouldn't have . . . and he was terrified.'

Too bad for him, thought the inspector. And since he now felt rather far away from this whole story, he changed the subject.

'Did you know that in Genoa I ran into a girlfriend of Trincanato's, and the encounter set off a big row with Livia?'

'Tell me, tell me.'

*

He felt bored to death being holed up at home. He didn't know how to make the time pass.

At five o'clock Fazio rang to tell him there was no news.

At six, Zito's secretary called to inform him, urgently, that the Finance Police were still going through the books and that Nicolò had been unable to go on the air. For the time being, there was no way they could do the interview. Then – but only because time seemed to be standing still – he thought back on what Ingrid had told him. Maybe, since he had nothing else to do at the moment, turning his mind briefly to Trincanato might be a good way to make the hours pass.

Right. But how?

Ever since he'd been forced to act like a fugitive, he was no longer able to go around questioning people and seeking information. Nor could he avail himself of Fazio's services.

So much for that idea.

He was condemned to idleness. And he didn't feel like reading.

He spent half an hour in front of the French windows to the veranda – though standing far enough back so that nobody outside could see him – looking through a pair of binoculars at the trawlers returning to the harbour.

*

At eight o'clock, since he still didn't feel hungry, he sat down in the armchair and turned on the television.

On the Free Channel, the screen was filled with a notice saying that due to a technical malfunction the news programme had been postponed but would return to the airwaves as soon as possible.

He clicked on TeleVigàta. Pippo Ragonese's chicken-arse face appeared on the screen. He looked rather upset.

Just minutes ago we received news that we've barely had time to confirm. The well-known business executive Giovanni Trincanato has been found dead at his home in Vigàta.

For a moment, Montalbano became a hyperrealist sculpture: *Seated Man Watching Television*. Then the first thing that came into his head was the thought that Trincanato now had nothing more to be afraid of. Not the most Christian of thoughts, clearly. But Trincanato didn't deserve any better.

The body was discovered by Antonietta Cipolla, the housekeeper, who had taken the afternoon off to visit her ailing sister.

Trincanato's second housekeeper had also been absent, having requested six hours' leave, from six p.m. to midnight. So far the cause of the death remains unknown.

At this point the outside of Trincanato's house appeared on the screen. Montalbano recognized the cars belonging to the forensics lab, Dr Pasquano, the prosecutor, and Gallo. Which meant that he'd died a violent death, and it was the Vigàta Police who were investigating.

With the heaviest of hearts, and feeling more melancholy than angry, he realized that he'd been left out in the cold. In the past he would have vented his rage by trashing the TV; but now, perhaps because of his age, he didn't even have the strength to curse the saints.

Ragonese returned on screen, holding a sheet of paper.

We've just now learned that the cause of Trincanato's death was murder. Apparently he was killed with one bullet shot to the base of the skull. If this news is confirmed, appearances would indicate the hand of the Mafia behind this act. The investigation is being led by Inspector Virginio Stracquadanio, who is replacing – definitively, it would seem, according to leaks from the commissioner's office – Inspector Salvo Montalbano as the head of the Vigàta commissariat.

A hand with another sheet of paper appeared in a corner of the screen. Ragonese took the sheet, looked at it, then said:

The plot thickens. It turns out that a man has been found bound and gagged in one of the servants' rooms of Palazzo Trincanato. He would appear to be the businessman's personal chauffeur. At this point we have deemed it best not to follow the programme schedule initially planned for this evening. In its place we will broadcast a TV film, which we'll interrupt periodically for updates as they come in.

Montalbano got up, went and got the whisky bottle, a glass, a pack of cigarettes, and his lighter, arranged them all next to the armchair, and sat back down.

. . . replacing – definitively, it would seem, according to leaks from the commissioner's office . . .

He felt his forehead. It was hot. He must have developed a mild fever.

He poured himself half a glass, and downed it in a single gulp.

. . . according to leaks . . .

Leaks, my arse.

Hizzoner the C'mishner had taken advantage of the opportunity to broadcast far and wide that, as far as the police were concerned, Inspector Salvo Montalbano, as of that moment, could go and sell chicory or chickpeas on a street corner, according to his preference.

. . . replacing – definitively, it would seem . . .

He couldn't stand watching the television any longer. On the screen were two comics who were unlikely, at such a moment, to make him laugh . . .

He was about to get up when Ragonese reappeared.

We ask our viewing audience to stay tuned to this channel, because Inspector Stracquadanio has told us he is available to grant us an interview in about twenty minutes. So we'll be back shortly. Meanwhile, we shall now suspend the broadcast of the TV film and show you the first images of the total eclipse of the moon.

Eclipse? He hadn't heard any mention of it. Refilling his glass, he got up, went out on the veranda, and sat down. After all, if he kept the outside light off, nobody could see him. Anyway, at this point, even if somebody did see him, what could they do?

It was true: the moon was in eclipse.

Already a quarter of the moon had been cancelled by a dense black blot.

To him the moon had always looked like a cheerful face. And it still did now, despite the fact that part of it had been chewed off.

He went inside, found his binoculars, and sat back down on the veranda.

At that point he noticed a column of ants on the veranda's wooden balustrade. What brought the column, which was moving, to his attention was the fact that it came to a sudden halt, as if on command.

Why did the ants all suddenly stop and stay that way, not making the slightest move?

Could they possibly have all died at once?

He brought the tip of his index finger close to one and touched it lightly. The insect moved a millimetre or two and then froze again.

Montalbano felt a cold shiver run down his spine. The temperature was dropping, in tandem with the lunar eclipse.

He finished his glass and went down to the beach, bringing the binoculars with him. He noticed that the sand felt freezing cold.

He reached the water's edge.

There was a gentle surf, but it was as if there was none. The water was moving so slowly and softly that it made no sound at all.

It was getting darker and darker.

Two crabs of the kind that usually hide under the sand were now moving around out in the open, one beside the other, as though giving each other courage.

Everything seemed to have stopped, waiting for the moon to disappear.

And why could he not even hear any distant sounds? A car's engine? A dog barking?

The inspector then lay on the cold sand, stomach up, and looked through the binoculars.

Not much of the moon was left, but the tiny remaining sliver seemed indifferent to what was happening.

Then there was only a black disc in the sky. Or a vast, bottomless hole in the universe. Mildly frightened, Montalbano closed his eyes.

The Great Cemeteries Under the Moon was the title of a book by a French author he'd read many years before.

But the great cemetery the world around him had become a few minutes earlier didn't even have the comfort of the moon.

The chills running down his spine became more frequent.

He slowly reopened his eyes. The nightmare was almost over.

Now it was the moon that was annulling the black disc.

And it had the same expression as before the eclipse. Perhaps because this had happened to it so many times before over the centuries that it no longer even noticed.

You should feel heartened by the moon, the inspector told himself . . . Or by Brecht, who said that however long the night might be, it will never be eternal.

Far away a dog barked.

Life was resuming after an interruption, a pause, a moment of nonlife.

He sat up. The crabs were gone. They'd been quick to carve out new lairs under the sand, and surely the column of ants on the balustrade had resumed running back and forth.

He lay back down.

He watched the moon through the binoculars until it was full again, bright and whole as before.

And at that very moment, before his eyes, silhouetted against the moon like a Chinese shadow puppet or some cinematic special effect, there began to appear, ever so slowly, first the foremast, then, little by little, the entire profile of a large sailing ship. A schooner.

Majestic and solemn, it crossed the field of light with sails unfurled and quivering with a wind that seemed to have risen just for it.

Then it vanished.

Montalbano remained spellbound.

Had he hallucinated, or had he just seen the *Halcyon*?

*

He went home and sat back down in the armchair, just in time to hear Ragonese saying:

> *We will now broadcast the interview that Inspector Stracquadanio so kindly granted our reporter, Filiberto Savasta.*

Stracquadanio looked about forty, with a well-toned physique and an intelligent look in his eye. Montalbano did not find him unlikeable. Stracquadanio began speaking without waiting to be asked by the journalist.

> *First, I would like to report the facts as they stand. At around half-past six this evening two individuals rang the buzzer outside the home of Giovanni Trincanato, who had been indisposed for the past few days and had not left the house. The men identified themselves as police officers and asked to*

speak to him. Michele Zaccaria, Trincanato's chauffeur, who'd answered the intercom because the housekeepers were away, then went into Trincanato's bedroom to inform him of the visit. His employer told him to let the two officers in and to stay with them while he got dressed. The chauffeur opened the door, looked out from the landing, and saw the two purported officers putting on ski masks and taking out handguns. They ordered Zaccaria to remain silent. A moment later he fell to the ground unconscious, struck in the back of the head with a pistol butt. It is assumed that the two men then went looking for Trincanato, found him in his bedroom still getting dressed, and killed him with one shot to the base of the skull. One of the housekeepers found the body upon returning at eight o'clock.

Reporter: Excuse me for interrupting, but isn't a shot to the base of the skull a hallmark of the Mafia?

Stracquadanio: Yes. And so?

Reporter: Well, it seems clear to me –

Stracquadanio: – that this is a Mafia crime? I think you're relying too much on appearances.

Reporter: What do you mean?

Stracquadanio: I mean just what I said. Appearances don't always correspond with reality.

Reporter: So are you ruling out that it could be a Mafia crime?

Stracquadanio: At this point I'm not ruling anything out. I will call to your attention, however, that less than a month ago Mr Trincanato had been subjected to some severe intimidation, for which the carabinieri ended up arresting two people.

Reporter: So do you think, perhaps, that the crime is in some way related to Mr Trincanato closing his business? That it might be the act of an exasperated worker?

Stracquadanio: However hard I try, I cannot remember ever coming across a case of workers killing someone who gave them work. It is true, however, that the closing of a business like Trincanato's definitely brings with it grave repercussions for the company.

Reporter: So the investigation will be oriented towards—

Stracquadanio: Thank you, I've nothing more to say.

Smart kid, no doubt about it.

The doorbell rang. Before opening, he looked through the peephole.

It was Fazio. He opened the door.

'How come Stracquadanio let you go free?'

Fazio was frowning darkly.

'I've been free the whole time. Mr Inspector didn't see

fit to include me in the investigation team. No doubt following orders.'

They sat on the veranda.

'What's Stracquadanio like?' asked Montalbano.

'He seems like a good kid. A bit out of his element. The force isn't really cooperating with him.'

'How would he take it if you went and told him a few things?'

'I dunno, but I can try and see.'

'Feel up to it?'

'Sure. What do you want me to tell him?'

'The first thing to tell him is that Trincanato was expecting something like this. He was holed up at home not because he was ill, but because he was scared to death. He realized that he'd said too much one time when he'd had too much to drink.'

'And what did he say?'

'I don't know. But I got it from a reliable source.'

'Anything else?'

'Yes, and important to boot. The killers' intention was to kill only Trincanato, and in fact they spared the chauffeur. Do you agree?'

'Completely.'

'Do you agree that if they'd found themselves faced with the two housekeepers, they would have been forced to commit a massacre?'

'Yep.'

'And that's why they wanted to do the deed when the housekeepers were out. One had actually left just half an hour before they got there. So the question is this: who informed the killers?'

Fazio thought about this for a moment. 'It could only have been the chauffeur.'

'Right. And he had them club him in the head so he could have an alibi. You have to tell Stracquadanio to squeeze him hard. Unless he comes to the same conclusion himself.'

'Maybe it's best to give him a little push anyway.'

The telephone rang. At that hour it could only be Livia. At any rate, just to be safe, Montalbano disguised his voice.

'Hello?'

'Salvo, is that you?'

He recognized Nicolò Zito's voice, and turned on the speakerphone.

'Hello, Nicolò. What is it?'

'There's big news. The commissioner called me in for questioning.'

'Have you gone yet?'

'I'm just coming out now.'

'What did he want?'

'At first he spoke to me gently and politely. He begged me not to broadcast our interview, or to wait at least a week. Then he said, and these were his exact words: "You'll see for yourself that there was no point in broadcasting it." '

'And what did you say?'

'I countered with the usual argument about the freedom

of the press, but he said he was in no way enforcing any censorship. And he added, the bastard, that if the Finance Police's inspection lasted another week, it wasn't his fault.'

'So, in other words, he was blackmailing you.'

'Exactly.'

'What do you think you'll do?'

'I'm in a delicate position, Salvo. Somebody – clearly someone from the commissioner's office – informed the Free Channel that the tug-of-war between us and them was due to your interview. And since we lose tons of money for every day of broadcasting we miss, you can imagine if this thing drags on for a while longer. Long story short, I risk getting fired.'

Montalbano didn't have to think twice.

'Call the commissioner right now and accept his one-week postponement.'

'Thank you,' said Nicolò, hanging up.

ELEVEN

The moment he woke up, the first thing that came into his mind from the night before was the image of the *Halcyon* passing in front of the moon with sails unfurled. But was it really the *Halcyon,* or just another ship that closely resembled it? He decided to have a look.

First, however, he needed to do something he'd been thinking about in depth ever since Fazio left.

Enough of chess games, of moves and countermoves. For whatever reason, he felt as if the eclipse had been a kind of message, a signal that he hadn't fully understood but which was enough to make him change tack.

If the commissioner had the right to do what he was doing, he, too, had the right, indeed the duty, to defend himself openly. Because this involved not only his prior career – since he didn't give a shit about his future one – but also, and above all, his dignity as a man.

He got up and opened the window. It was a beautiful, sunny day, which didn't hurt. He filled his lungs with good fresh air, washed and dressed, drank three cups of coffee, lolled about the house waiting for nine o'clock to come round, then strode with determination over to the phone and dialled the number.

'Hello? Inspector Montalbano here. I would like to speak to the commissioner.'

'Please hold.'

He didn't have time to count to ten.

'Montalbano? Did I get that right?'

'Yes.'

'Where are you calling from?'

Bonetti-Alderighi seemed neither surprised nor angry. Before answering, Montalbano took a deep breath, then dived in. 'From Vigàta.'

'You were right to phone me. I was about to call you myself. Did you want to tell me something?'

Something? A whole mountain of things! He felt the rage returning but was able to control it by taking another deep breath.

'I never actually gave that interview.'

This time it was the commissioner who paused.

'I already knew that. And I also knew you were in Vigàta.'

Montalbano staggered, feeling blindsided. What kind of game was Bonetti-Alderighi playing?

'You knew the interview didn't exist even before calling in the Finance Police?'

'Yes.'

'Then why did you do it?'

'Try and understand, Montalbano. I needed to make

some noise, to call attention to the friction between you and me.'

Had he gone mad? 'Listen, Mr Commissioner—'

'Montalbano, don't you think it would be better to talk in person?'

'I agree. I'll be right over.'

'Then you haven't understood a thing! You absolutely must not be seen at Montelusa Central! If any journalist gets wind of the fact that you're still in touch with me, then all the work I've done will have been for naught!'

'But I really need to—'

'Let's do this. I'll send a van over straightaway to pick you up. Ah, I almost forgot. To avoid any further misunderstandings I should tell you that just a short while ago I issued a communiqué stating that you have been removed from the force. See you in a bit.'

Montalbano felt dazed, shaken, numb. Had he been removed from the force or not? Should he raise hell or not? To clear his head, he drank half a glass of whisky and two more coffees.

Then somebody rang at the door, and he went to answer.

Right there in front of the house was a police van with its rear doors already open.

'Get inside so I can close it up,' said the uniformed cop who'd rung the doorbell.

Montalbano locked the house and climbed in. The back doors closed with a dry crack, and the cop settled in behind the wheel and drove off.

As soon as they were past Vigàta, Montalbano was assailed by a suspicion that drenched him in sweat.

Was this all a feint on the part of the commissioner? A trap? What if Bonetti-Alderighi had tricked him into getting into the van just to take him to some isolated place and hold him prisoner?

But did he have the power to do that? Why not, if he could so easily get the Finance Police involved?

At any rate, now there was nothing to be done about it. He'd fallen for it like a fool and had to accept the consequences.

Looking out of the only window, a narrow slit with bars, he saw that they were entering the courtyard of Montelusa Central Police. What a relief. No captivity at the bottom of a well. The worst they could do was put him in a holding cell.

The van stopped, the doors opened. 'Please follow me,' said the cop.

They were in the internal car park, but he didn't see anyone about. They'd definitely all been cleared out to make way for his arrival. He followed the officer, who opened the lift door for him.

'Top floor, first door on the right. Goodbye,' he said.

The inspector had never been up to the top floor before. He knew there was an apartment there, reserved for high-profile guests. He went into the first door on the right.

The space was furnished as a small sitting room. He went over to a window. There was a lovely view. The Vigàta sea looked as if you could reach out and touch it with your hand.

'Montalbano, my good man!'

It was Bonetti-Alderighi, coming towards him with a smile on his lips and holding his hand out after closing the door.

The inspector shook his hand robotically.

'Please sit down. We can speak openly here without worry.'

Unable to restrain himself, Montalbano spoke first. 'If you don't mind, before anything I'd like to know the reason for my removal from the force,' he said brusquely.

'Oh, that? It's the icing on the cake.'

Icing, my arse.

'Please explain.'

The commissioner looked at him and realized he shouldn't draw things out.

'I'll tell you the whole story from the start. It began even before you received that letter from the personnel office, which I'd requested, forcing you to take a holiday.'

'So the letter was fake?' Montalbano burst out.

'No, of course it wasn't fake. You've accumulated so many days of leave it's frightening, but in fact it was me, as I said, who requested the letter.'

'Why?'

'Montalbano, would you please be so kind as not to interrupt me with your questions?'

'Sorry.'

'Over a month ago, I was informed of the imminent arrival of an important person from the FBI, with orders to make myself completely available to him. As soon as this agent got here – oh, and I should mention, incidentally, that he's Sicilian American and his name is Jack Pennisi – the first thing he asked me was to make it so that everyone thought that you'd been dismissed and those who'd always worked most closely with you were being reassigned elsewhere. Naturally, it was all just a ruse.'

Montalbano felt so confused, it was as if he had two big flies buzzing inside his ears.

'But was it Pennisi himself who brought up my name?' he asked, wide-eyed.

'None other. I was as surprised as you are.'

'But how did the FBI know that I even existed?'

'I have no idea, but I guess they're pretty well informed. He also told me that you had to remain temporarily in the dark about his request. I explained to him that I would need a little time, that I could only proceed in stages, and he replied that he could only grant me a month. And so I had personnel send you that letter. As soon as you went away, I sprang into action, transferring Inspector Augello and spreading the rumour that you would no longer be the chief of the Vigàta commissariat. But you know what, Montalbano? I was hoping for a more extreme reaction on your part. It would have made my task easier. Anyway, I then issued the communiqué announcing your dismissal.'

Montalbano was still having serious doubts about what the commissioner was telling him. Deep down he didn't believe him. It sounded like a wild American fantasy, like those spy movies with plots so complicated he never understood a thing.

'Fake, naturally.'

'The dismissal? Of course.'

'Will you believe me, Mr Commissioner, if I say I'm very perplexed? On the one hand, I'm pleased with what you've just told me, but on the other, I'm wondering about the reason for all this playacting. What's the endgame?'

The commissioner threw up his hands.

'I can't help you there. Believe me. Even I don't know; they didn't tell me. I hope, in any case, that this clears things up for you.'

And he reached into his jacket pocket, pulled out a sealed envelope, and handed it to the inspector.

'This is for you. It arrived last night from the Ministry of Justice.'

It was a normal-looking manila envelope without any letterhead. On it was written: '*For Inspector Salvo Montalbano. To be opened and read in private.*'

'I have nothing more to tell you,' said the commissioner, getting up and shaking his hand. 'Take the lift back down. You'll be escorted home in the same manner as before. Best of luck.'

The man who got into the lift and then into the van was not Inspector Montalbano, even if he looked just like him, but an effigy, a double, an identical replicant who moved mechanically.

Because his brain had short-circuited and was now emitting smoke as it rattled around in his skull.

*

The same Montalbano robot, as soon as he got home, took his clothes off, put his trunks on, and dived into the sea. Even though it was late May and the water was still cold.

He swam for an hour, and when he returned to shore his brain was working again.

'Adelì, you don't need to make anything for lunch. I'm going to go out to eat.'

He got dressed, sat down on the veranda, and opened the envelope.

Instructions. To be followed to the letter.

1. Beginning today, 25 May, you must go to an estate agency in Vigàta and put your Marinella home up for sale. You must also arrange to affix a FOR SALE sign near your house, in a place visible from the main road. You needn't worry. This is only for show.
2. As of this moment, you must have no more contact whatsoever with Montelusa Central Police.
3. You should make known to as many people as possible your violent rancour towards the police force, for their patently ungenerous treatment of you. But you must not give any televised or print interviews.
4. Keep a packed suitcase ready for being away no more than ten days.
5. Let everyone know that you intend to return to Boccadasse as soon as possible.
6. On 27 May, sometime over the course of the day a

person you do not know will contact you. You will follow his orders. You must therefore stay at home for that whole day.

7. Your second-in-command and your assistant will play marginal roles in the operation. They will be informed of their tasks at the proper time.
8. You must always answer your telephone.
9. Burn these instructions.
10. Do not speak about any of this with anyone, not even your girlfriend, Livia.

The letter was not signed. The American God had sent him the new Decalogue. Two points in particular had struck him. The one about packing a suitcase and the one about not mentioning anything to Livia.

He flicked on his lighter to burn the sheet of paper, but then changed his mind and lit a cigarette with the flame instead. The sheet he hid inside the pages of a novel.

'See you tomorrow, Adelì.'

He'd been right. Just as the moon had not been frightened by the eclipse because it knew it was just a momentary thing, likewise he shouldn't be too worried about the situation, since he knew it was temporary.

He decided to have faith. He got in the car and headed for Vigàta.

The estate agency was still open. There was a pretty girl behind the counter.

'May I help you?' she asked, smiling.

'I'm the former Inspector Montalbano,' he said.

'I know you,' said the girl. 'But why former?'

'Didn't you know? I've been dismissed, indeed removed from the force.'

The girl's smile vanished. 'I'm sorry.'

'I'm not. At this point the place is filled with idiots. If anything should happen to you, I advise you to call the carabinieri, not the police.'

The girl said nothing.

'I would like to put my house in Marinella up for sale as soon as possible,' Montalbano continued.

'Selling too fast can mean getting less for—'

'I know, but I don't care. I would like my signs starting today.'

'Will you be at home around four o'clock this afternoon?'

'Yes.'

'Mr Giuliano will come to value the property and take the details. Please have the title deeds of the property available for him.'

'Thank you. Would you like the address?'

'No, we know where it is. But let me have your telephone number.'

Point number I had been done.

*

'Is the news really true?' Enzo asked him as soon as he came into the trattoria.

'What news?'

'That you were thrown off the force.'

'It's true.'

'But why?'

Enzo seemed genuinely distressed.

Three or four customers who knew the inspector turned and looked. He answered Enzo's question in a loud voice so that everyone could hear him.

'How should I know? All I know is that they're a bunch of bastards who deserve only to be spat at. In the face. Let's drop the subject, Enzo, or it's going to spoil my appetite. That's something they haven't succeeded in taking away from me yet.'

He'd just finished eating a big dish of spaghetti with seafood and had already started on his mullet when Enzo came and said there was a phone call for him.

'Did they say who they were?'

'Yes, sir, it's Inspector Stracquadanio.'

'Tell him to call back in fifteen minutes.'

He wanted to finish his mullet in peace and at the same time make it publicly clear just how pissed off he was.

Stracquadanio was punctual.

'Hello, Montalbano, I'm sorry we have to meet this way at such an unfortunate moment, but . . .'

'Go ahead.'

'Could you come in here this afternoon to clear out your desk?'

Though he knew it was all a put-on, a hoax, he felt terrible just the same.

'All right, tomorrow morning I—'

'No, you should come this afternoon. It's what the commissioner wants.'

What did the commissioner have to do with this?

All at once he understood. Stracquadanio had something he needed to tell him. The business about the desk was just a pretext.

'All right, I'll be there around five-thirty.' He went and sat back down.

'Enzo, could you bring me another serving of mullet?'

*

A walk along the jetty was a dire necessity, so weighted down was his belly.

Already from a distance he could see that there was no sign of the *Halcyon* at the docks. And yet he was almost certain that what he'd seen the night before was the schooner's silhouette.

The usual fisherman was in his usual spot. Montalbano stopped.

'Hello.'

'Hello, Inspector.'

'I'm not an inspector anymore.'

'Did you retire?'

'No, I got kicked out.'

'Oh.'

'Did the *Halcyon* put out to sea?'

The fisherman gave him a confused look.

'No, sir, there's been no sign of the *Halcyon*.'

Had he dreamt it?

*

Mr Giuliano of the estate agency was a hurried man of about forty. After a brief look at the deeds to the house, he went from room to room, said that they could ask for five hundred thousand euros but accept four hundred and fifty, had the inspector sign a paper, stuck a for sale sign with the agency's number on it beside the front door, then stuck another one into the ground at the end of the driveway, at the side of the provincial road.

They left it that they would get in touch with each other as soon as there was any news.

Immediately afterwards, Montalbano drove off to the Vigàta station with an empty suitcase in which to put the personal belongings from his desk.

Lost in thought, he walked right past the switchboard cupboard, charging on straight ahead.

'Excuse me – where are you going?' shouted a uniformed policeman.

'Sorry.'

'Who are you?'

'Montalbano. I have an appointment with Inspector Stracquadanio.'

'Please follow me.'

He opened the door to the waiting room.

'Please wait here,' he said, closing the door behind him.

Montalbano sat down in a small armchair, and it made

a threatening sound. So he got up and sat in the other small armchair. Which was worse than the first, if that was possible. As soon as he decided that it was best to wait standing, a bomb, or something similar, exploded in the room. Ears still ringing from the blast, he saw that the deafening noise had been made by the door opening suddenly and crashing against the wall. And there, in the doorway, was Catarella, standing at attention, looking at him and weeping as the tears streamed down his face and wet his collar and tie. He stood motionless for a few moments, then turned around and disappeared. Montalbano felt a great wave of emotion sweep over him, pulled out his handkerchief, and blew his nose.

Then Fazio appeared, panting heavily.

'I just found out you were here. What's going on? What's this about you being thrown off the force?'

'You have to make everyone think it's true.'

Fazio's face brightened.

'You mean it's not?!'

'Listen, this isn't the place to discuss this. Come to my house this evening.'

'Nine o'clock OK?'

'Nine o'clock's fine.'

Three minutes later the uniformed officer returned. 'The inspector's waiting for you.'

Stracquadanio greeted him with a smile, but seemed rather nervous.

'Forgive me for making you wait, Montalbano, but it's been total chaos here.'

'Meaning?'

'You've heard about the Trincanato murder?'

'Of course.'

'Well, I'd told the chauffeur, who was hospitalized immediately for the head injury he sustained when the killers broke in, to come in for questioning as soon as he was released. Which he was, today at four p.m. But he never came. Quite incredibly, he appears to have been kidnapped the moment he stepped out of the hospital.'

'Listen,' said Montalbano, 'I can see that you're too busy. I'll get out of your hair to let you work freely. I'll put my papers in this suitcase and . . .'

Stracquadanio gawked at him.

'But clearing your desk was just a pretext to make you come here!'

'To do what?'

'You must wait for a phone call. As per the commissioner's instructions.'

'A call from whom?'

'How should I know?'

TWELVE

Montalbano was starting to feel rather dumbfounded by all this atmosphere of secrecy, trips in the police van like a common criminal, imperative decalogues, and fake dismissals.

But he had no other choice than to be patient.

Stracquadanio was quite courteous and offered him a coffee. The curious thing, however, was that while they were waiting for the call, he carefully avoided mentioning the Trincanato murder, talking only about his own career. When at last the telephone rang, Stracquadanio passed Montalbano the receiver. He was about to leave the room when the inspector signalled for him to stay.

It was better to have a witness who could hear at least one half of the conversation.

'Montalbano here. Who is this?'

'Jack's the name. Jack Pennisi. Hello, *paisàn*. I guess you don't speak no American, right?

'Right.'

'Listen up, I wan' yiz t'get in yer car and come over 'ere straightaways-like, bu' wittout makin' a lotta racket.'

This FBI man spoke pure Sicilian dialect. 'Here meaning where?'

'Take the ol' road for Montelusa. After a level crossing, there's an unmade road. 'Bout a hunnert metres down 'iss road 'ere's an abandoned house. I'll be waitin' fer yiz inside.'

And of course he's going to wanna do it in a ramshackle old house! Otherwise it wouldn't be much of an American movie, now, would it?

'And what am I supposed to do there?'

'Once y'er there, you'll unnastand.'

'No, you must tell me now.'

'Don't you trust me?'

'It's not a question of trust. I don't even know you.'

'OK. Whatever you like. I got the chauffeur, Zaccaria, 'ere wit' me, an' I want you to interrogate 'im.'

Montalbano couldn't believe his ears.

'It was you who kidnapped the chauffeur?'

Stracquadanio, upon hearing these words, leapt up from his chair and just stood there, mouth agape.

'Yeah, righ' when 'e's comin' outta the hospital.'

At first Montalbano felt shocked, then troubled.

'Tell me something: do you think you can just come here and play if you catch a Turk, he's yours?'

The American chuckled.

'What's so funny?'

'Tha'ss som'n my grandpa use ta say to me whenever I stole a coupla cents outta his jacket.'

'Well, I'm asking the same question. Don't you know

that's something you can't just do here? That kidnapping is a serious crime? And you have no authority to act this way?'

'Yeah, I know.'

'But if you know, then why did you do it?'

''Cause I don't trust yer cops.'

Suddenly Montalbano, whose balls were already in a supersonic spin, saw red.

'Lemme tell you something. And I'll tell you just this once. The person interrogating Zaccaria has to be Inspector Stracquadanio of Vigàta. Is that clear?'

'So tha'ss the way it is?'

'Yes, sir, that's the way it is. And now you must arrange to drop Zaccaria off in front of our station within no more than half an hour. You are in Italy, and you must respect Italian laws.'

'An' wha'ss going to happen to me if I don'?' the American asked mockingly.

'What'll happen is that I'll have all the roads blocked in five minutes, and you'll be trapped like a rat in a cage.'

'You really mean that?'

'I really do.'

'But do you wanna work wit' me or not?'

'Yes, but in my own way. Or, at the very least, after we come to a mutual agreement.'

'Yeah, but Inspector What's-His-Name don't know what I wanna know about Zaccaria.'

'Then I'll put him on so you can explain the whole thing to him. Goodbye.'

He handed the receiver to Stracquadanio, who started talking American. To dispel his irritation, Montalbano went and opened the window, stuck his head out, and lit a cigarette.

Who the fuck did these Americans think they were? Masters of the world? Who could do whatever the hell they pleased in other people's homes?

You couldn't really say the collaboration with the FBI was off to a good start.

After Stracquadanio had finished speaking to Pennisi, Montalbano went over to him.

'Did you manage to understand any of what's going on?' he asked him.

'I think I'm starting to,' said Stracquadanio, giving him a funny look. 'But I don't want any explanations. And you should know that I intend to inform the commissioner of what happened and follow his instructions to the letter.'

'That's the right thing to do,' said Montalbano, picking up his suitcase. 'Come, it won't take me five minutes to empty my desk for you.'

'Wait a second,' said Stracquadanio. 'Can you tell me, if you know, what the *Halcyon* is?'

This, for Montalbano, was like a blow to the head. He sat back down, stunned.

So the FBI was interested in the ship? He needed to confirm this.

'Why do you ask?'

'The American wants to know what its next port of call will be. He says the chauffeur definitely knows and it is of capital importance that he tell us. But I don't think it'll be so easy to get this Zaccaria to talk. He seemed to me like a pretty tough customer.'

'The *Halcyon* is a large, mysterious pleasure schooner, which Trincanato supplied with victuals and hookers. That's all I can tell you, really. As for the chauffeur, if you want my advice, you should threaten to turn him back over to the American. He'll shit his pants, you'll see.'

☼

Half an hour after he got back home, Fazio rang. 'Chief, I can't come to your place.'

'Why not?'

''Cause Inspector Stracquadanio wants me to stick around while he interrogates Zaccaria.'

'So he's at the station?'

'Yeah, he got here about five minutes ago.'

Good. Pennisi had been persuaded and hadn't had any brilliant ideas of his own.

'Well, let's leave it that if Stracquadanio manages to end the interrogation before midnight, you come here afterwards; otherwise I'll see you tomorrow.'

☼

While he waited for his appetite to return, he sat down and turned on the television:

> *. . . which marks the inglorious end of the career of Inspector Montalbano . . .*

Ragonese was saying with a triumphant expression on his face.

> *We can only applaud this rightful, though overdue measure taken by Commissioner Bonetti-Alderighi . . .*

He changed channels and started watching a cowboy movie that grew stale after fifteen minutes.

He turned the set off, got up, laid the table on the veranda, and regaled himself with Adelina's *sartù* and *parmigiana.*

The phone rang. It was Livia, in a quasi-hysterical state.

'But is it true? Is it true?'

'Is what true?'

'That you've been fired!'

'Who told you that?'

'Beba called and told me. She was very upset. Is it true?'

He had to calm her down.

'No, not exactly. I had a pretty bad run-in with the commissioner, and in the end he requested my dismissal. But it's just a request, got that? A heartfelt wish. Which doesn't necessarily mean that it'll come to anything, especially because I will oppose it.'

It took a good half-hour to convince her.

He was about to go to bed, as it was past twelve thirty, when the doorbell rang. It was Fazio.

'Zaccaria spilled the beans. That Stracquadanio's really good.'

'Did he have you witness the interrogation?'

'Witness, no, but when it was over he told me everything and said I should come here and tell you.'

'So tell me.'

Fazio made a little smirk. 'Nah.'

'Why not?'

'Because first you have to tell me exactly what is going on. What? You're thrown off the force, which practically gave me a temperature, Catarella's crying his eyes out, half the force is up in arms and wants to write a letter of protest, and then Stracquadanio, just like that, orders me to tell you everything in detail as though nothing had ever happened?'

'Are you blackmailing me?'

'Yes, sir, I am.'

Montalbano told him about his meeting with the commissioner.

'I just knew something was up!' said Fazio, heaving a sigh of relief.

The inspector then stood up, went over and got the Americans' Ten Commandments, and had Fazio read them.

'So we're supposed to be at the FBI's disposal?' Fazio asked when he'd finished.

'So it seems. Now it's your turn to talk.'

'I'll start with the murder of Trincanato. One day Trincanato got a phone call from the captain of the *Halcyon*, which was on its way to Genoa. The captain told him he wanted Fantuzzo, Trincanato's bodyguard, to be sent to Genoa, then added that he wouldn't be needing the usual supplies of food and girls for the next journey, because they'd decided to call at a different port.'

'Wait a second. Did Zaccaria say what the purpose of the *Halcyon* is?'

'Yes, it's a floating casino. A gambling ship for billionaires with bottomless pockets from all over the world. There is no monetary limit on the bets wagered, and they gamble day and night. The girls are available to whoever wants them.'

Montalbano remembered Zito's broadcast.

'I get it. Something similar to what goes on in some of those Kenyan casinos.'

'No, Chief, this is different. For better or worse, in Kenya there are at least some rules. And there are many, many players. On the *Halcyon,* on the other hand, there are no rules, there are few players, and, most importantly, the casino opens after the schooner enters international waters, where nobody has any power.'

'But where do the players board the ship?'

'Remember when we were speculating about that? Well, it turns out we were right. They board sometimes from obscure African ports, or else at sea from their own yachts.'

'Go on.'

'Well, upon hearing this news, Trincanato got pissed off. And worried that they didn't want his services anymore.'

'But what did he get out of it?'

'For one thing, they apparently paid him well for his trouble. Then every so often they would let him on board for free, because the price of admission to a club that exclusive, and only for fifteen days, is extremely high, the kind of thing only real billionaires can afford. Then, you can imagine, with all those beautiful girls passing through his hands, he certainly took advantage of the situation . . .'

'So what did he do?'

'He made such a fuss, phoning everyone in protest, that one day somebody arrived here from Bolivia and explained to him that it was just a temporary situation, but involved something very important, after which everything would go back to the way it was before.'

'And did he tell him what this temporary situation involved?'

'In so many words. But he ordered him to remain silent.'

'And instead Trincanato let a few things slip one evening after he'd been drinking . . .'

'Exactly. And at that point Fantuzzo, who was there, informed the organization. And they told him to kill him immediately. It was him and Zaccaria who got rid of him, taking advantage of the fact that the housekeepers were out, as you'd said. And now everybody's looking for Fantuzzo.'

'Did Zaccaria reveal where the *Halcyon* will call next?'

'Yes, at Fiacca. It's stopping for supplies of food and drink, but no girls this time.'

'Has it ever called at Fiacca before?'

'No, this is the first time.'

'Wait a second. If this is the first time, who did they get to order the stuff?'

'Zaccaria.'

'And did he do it?'

'No, he didn't have time.'

'Tell me something. Where is Zaccaria right now?'

'At Montelusa Central.'

'And why isn't he in jail and made available to the prosecutor for questioning?'

'Commissioner's orders.'

'How much do you want to bet that at this very moment he's back with Pennisi, the FBI guy, who's probably skinning him alive?'

'Since I don't like to lose, I'm not going to take that bet. But what else would he want to know?'

'At least two things. The first is where Fantuzzo is hiding, so he can neutralize him.'

'You mean arrest him for the murder of Trincanato?'

'Pennisi doesn't give a fuck about Trincanato's murder. He just doesn't want Fantuzzo to get in touch with the *Halcyon* people. And be careful: for you the verb "neutralize" means "arrest"; for Pennisi it may well mean something else.'

'And the second thing?'

'Confirmation of what the FBI suspects.'

'Which is what?'

'Think, Fazio. What could this temporary but important and ever-so-secret situation the *Halcyon* is needed for be? So important, you'll remember, that the moment Trincanato talked about it, he was killed?'

It didn't take Fazio long.

'Maybe for transporting some very special stuff . . .

or maybe for a top-secret meeting completely out of everyone's sight?'

'Good guess. The second one, I mean. The right word for it would be "summit". A summit nobody is supposed to know anything about. To the point that this time they're not bringing any women on board. They don't want any witnesses. How much you want to bet that's what it is?'

'I repeat: I don't like losing.'

*

Sometime around half-past eight the next morning, just as he was finishing getting dressed, the doorbell rang. And since he hadn't slept well, he still felt muddleheaded. It couldn't be Adelina, since she had the keys. He went and opened the door. Before him stood a man of about forty, rather well dressed. He'd come in a fine, brand-new car, beside which his own car looked like a beggar's.

'Can I help you?'

'Is this the house for sale?'

Montalbano was at a loss.

'What?'

'Is this the house for sale?' the man repeated.

'What on earth . . .!' said the inspector, slamming the door in his face.

Then he froze. He'd completely forgotten he'd put the house on the market!

He reopened the door. The man was still there in front of him, standing stiff as a board. Montalbano decided to put on a little show so that the prospective buyer wouldn't change his mind.

'I'm sorry. I'm a little deaf. My age, don't you know . . . And how old are you?'

'Forty-one!'

'Lucky man! I, too, was once forty-one! So, you were saying?'

'I was asking if this is the house for sale,' said the man, beginning to lose patience.

'Ah, the house! I didn't quite get what you were saying. I thought you were saying something about mouse tail, and so . . . I've been having some problems with mice lately . . . they're very cute and all, but, you know . . . So, just to be clear, I'm ready to sell, because I'm forced to for reasons beyond my control. The bad turns life does a man sometimes, you know . . . So I have to sell the house, but these mice, well, I just don't know what to do about them! They're not why I'm selling, of course, but still . . .'

And he stared wildly at the sea.

The man must have thought he was dealing with a madman capable of anything.

So he looked at his watch, said it was getting late, promised to return, said goodbye, got back in his car, and sped away.

Montalbano didn't have time to close the door before he saw Adelina arrive, waving her arms in the air like a messenger in a Greek tragedy and wailing loudly.

'Wha' a shame! Wha' a shame!'

'What happened?'

'Is it true you was trown outta the police? Is it true you're leaving? Is it true you're sellin' your house?'

'It's true, but I've put in an appeal. The last word hasn't been said yet. So don't worry.'

'I'll have 'em say a novena to San Calò so you win your appeal!'

'All right, but bear one thing in mind, Adelì. This whole business has not made me lose my appetite. On the contrary. What are you going to make for me tonight?'

'*Pasta 'ncasciata.*'

'Will you teach me how to make it?'

Why not? He didn't have anything better to do . . .

'Sure. Bu' first I gotta tidy uppa the house. Go an' a take yisself a walk an' come a back in a hour.'

*

When he got back, Adelina told him there'd just been a call from the estate agents and she'd written the number down next to the phone.

'Hello?' said the pretty girl who worked at the agency, whose voice the inspector recognized.

'Montalbano here.'

'Thank you for calling back Insp – er, sir. A client of ours would like to see your house, and if you don't mind, he'll be accompanied by Mr Giuliano. Is this afternoon at four o'clock all right with you?'

'That's fine with me.'

It didn't take him long to learn how to make *pasta 'ncasciata* and, while they were at it, *melanzane alla parmigiana.*

He could now add those to all the other dishes Adelina had taught him in the past.

If he really did get thrown off the force, he thought, he could always open a Sicilian restaurant in Boccadasse.

*

He was early at Enzo's, not knowing what else to do at home after Adelina's lesson. He was the only customer.

Enzo was watching TeleVigàta. The one o'clock news was about to begin.

'Does it bother you?'

'No, no, please leave it on.'

'Want me to bring you some really fresh antipasti?'

'Bring it!'

The news programme logo came on, and then Pippo Ragonese's face appeared, beaming with the importance of the occasion.

> *There have been some major new developments in the Trincanato murder case. We were unaware that an arrest warrant had been issued for Ernesto Fantuzzo, the businessman's former bodyguard, who disappeared from circulation after the murder. Well, just minutes ago, we were told that Fantuzzo met his death in an exchange of gunfire with the Catturandi, the Organized Crime Unit of the national police, early this morning in the Magliocco district. This information has been confirmed by the police commissioner's office in Montelusa. We still have no details of the incident, but will promptly report them to our viewers as soon as we do. And now for other*

news, after which we will broadcast a brief interview granted us by Inspector Stracquadanio, the brilliant new head of the police commissariat of Vigàta.

Montalbano set to the antipasti and stopped listening to the news.

Not until Ragonese returned did he prick his ears up again.

THIRTEEN

We will now broadcast the exclusive interview granted us by Inspector Stracquadanio, said Ragonese.

The chicken-arse face disappeared, and in its place appeared an image of the Vigàta Police station car park. Stracquadanio was standing beside a squad car.

Reporter: Was it Zaccaria, Trincanato's chauffeur, who put you on Fantuzzo's trail?

Stracquadanio: Absolutely not. Zaccaria didn't recognize either of the two attackers. In addition, they were both wearing ski masks and didn't open their mouths during the entire operation. It was Fantuzzo's behaviour that first aroused our suspicions.

Reporter: Why, how did he act?

Stracquadanio: Well, he was Trincanato's bodyguard, wasn't he? And yet he was absent on the day of the murder; he hadn't come into work and didn't answer his phone. Once the crime was discovered, we sought him for questioning, but he'd precipitously moved out of his residence. We did, however, recover a ski mask at his home, and we think it might have been used in the attack on Trincanato's house with an accomplice.

Reporter: Is it true that the weapon found in Fantuzzo's hand was the same one used to kill Trincanato?

Stracquadanio: You're getting ahead of yourself. A superficial examination does show that the weapon is compatible with the preliminary findings, and the calibre is apparently the same. But we'll have to wait for the results of the ballistics tests, which are currently in progress.

Reporter: Has the accomplice been identified?

Stracquadanio: At the present stage of the investigation, I'd rather not answer that question.

Reporter: Can you tell us exactly where the chauffeur Zaccaria figures in all this?

Stracquadanio: Any involvement on his part in the murder is to be strictly ruled out. Zaccaria was questioned at great length as a witness. All his statements have been checked out and verified as true. Nothing whatsoever has emerged that could be held against him.

Ragonese's face returned. Montalbano couldn't stand it. Even his voice was unbearable.

He looked down and said to Enzo: 'Bring me another serving of antipasti, would you?'

No doubt about it, Stracquadanio was very skilful, not just as a policeman but also in front of a TV camera – something that usually turned him, Montalbano, into a babbling fool. There was also no doubt that Jack Pennisi went about things like a steamroller, but at the speed of a Formula I racing car. He had eliminated Fantuzzo, or arranged for his elimination, in record time. Who knew whether the whole business of the Organized Crime Unit and the firefight wasn't just a great big lie for public consumption?

He'd also managed to make Zaccaria seem as innocent as a cherub to the general public.

Apparently he still needed him for the plan he was preparing, then would leave him to his fate.

*

He'd just finished eating and was getting up to leave when the variety programme running on TeleVigàta was interrupted, and Ragonese's face reappeared.

We've just been informed of a shocking tragedy. A short while ago a number of foreign migrants landed at the port of Vigàta after being rescued at sea by our National Coast Guard. The seven castaways were found clinging for their lives to the wreck of a small barge. According to their account, there were no fewer than eighty of them, including women and children, when they set out from the Libyan coast, but they soon found themselves in an extremely dangerous predicament. At about two o'clock this morning, as they were heading for Italian shores just after passing through Maltese territorial waters, they crossed paths with a large sailing ship that not only refrained from lending them any assistance, but, in executing manoeuvres to distance itself from the barge, ended up colliding with it and sinking it. None of the survivors is able to tell us the name of the ship.

For whatever reason, Montalbano was certain that the sailing ship was the *Halcyon*.

Imagine those guys having time to waste on the wretched of the earth!

He could have sworn as well that the ramming had been intentional. The fewer witnesses to the *Halcyon*'s trafficking, the better. But they hadn't finished the job; seven migrants had been saved.

He felt so enraged that if he'd had the entire ship's crew within reach, he would have kicked each and every one's face in.

At any rate, any lingering doubts he might have had about collaborating with the FBI had vanished.

*

He prolonged his customary stroll along the jetty and his contemplative rest on the flat rock, either because the weather that day rated ten out of ten, or because he needed to occupy himself until he could return home shortly before four.

He barely had time to wash before the doorbell rang.

He went to answer.

It was Mr Giuliano with, beside him, a man in his mid-forties with a head like a cue ball, an ex-boxer's broken nose, blue eyes, a toothy smile, and the likable air of an open, honest gentleman.

'This is Mr Vincent Bonifacio,' said Giuliano, introducing him.

They all shook hands.

Mr Bonifacio's handshake nearly shattered the inspector's fingers.

'Please come in,' said Montalbano.

As they were entering, he asked: 'Shall I make you some coffee while you're looking at the house?'

Double affirmative.

Five minutes later Giuliano came in.

'Mr Bonifacio would like to take photos of the interior. Is that all right?'

'Of course.'

Fifteen minutes later they were all sitting out on the veranda with steaming demitasses in front of them.

'Mr Bonifacio,' Giuliano explained, 'lives in New York and would like to buy your house for his father, who is a native of Vigàta. That's why he took the photos, so he can send them to him.'

'And what do you do for a living in New York?' the inspector asked Bonifacio.

'I'm an *ondertecco*.'

Montalbano looked confusedly at Giuliano, who also seemed not to have understood. Then he asked Bonifacio:

'Undertaker?'

'Yes.'

'He owns a funeral home,' Giuliano said to the inspector.

'Not one, but five,' said Bonifacio. 'One in Brooklyn, one in Mulberry Street, one in—'

'Do you think the house might be right for your father?' the inspector asked, interrupting him.

'I think so. But what's certain is that I find it very appealing myself. I could spend the whole day sitting here like this, with the sea right in front of me! I'd pay a king's ransom to see the sunset!'

'As far as I'm concerned,' said the inspector, 'if you want to stay till sunset, you can be my guest . . . I'm relatively free, after all.'

'Really?' the American asked hopefully.

'The problem is that I have to go back into town,' interjected Giuliano, 'and you, Mr Bonifacio, left your car . . .'

'As far as that goes, it's not a problem,' Montalbano said readily. 'I can bring him back to town myself.'

'Thank you, thank you so much, you really are an exquisite person!' Bonifacio said in gratitude. 'You've given me an extra year of life!'

Giuliano stood up.

'So, what's the plan?' he asked Bonifacio.

'I'll come by your office tomorrow morning to sign the paper and make a deposit. OK?'

Montalbano saw Giuliano to the door, then went back to the American, who was still sitting on the veranda.

'I'd been wondering how you were going to make contact. As a prospective buyer of the house, however, is something I would never have imagined,' said Montalbano.

'How did you recognize me?'

'By your voice, the moment you opened your mouth. But tell me what your real name is.'

'Giacchino Pennisi, but everyone just calls me Jack.'

'Shall we continue with more coffee?'

'I'd rather with some Scotch on the rocks.'

Montalbano served him. He himself had another coffee, however. He wanted to keep his brain functioning properly.

'This really is a beautiful spot, you know. There's no commotion, no traffic, the air is clean, the beach is large . . .'

'Don't forget, the house isn't really for sale.'

Pennisi laughed.

'OK. Who's going to talk first, me or you?' asked Montalbano.

The American gave him a questioning look. 'Why, what do you know about this whole affair?'

'As far as knowing goes, nothing, but I have my own idea about it.'

'Let's hear it.'

'I'm convinced that the *Halcyon*, for the time being, is

no longer a floating casino, but is being used as the venue for a summit of some sort.'

'You're not going to tell me you came to that conclusion all on your own, are you?'

'Yes, I am.'

'What kind of summit?'

'Some kind of international summit between drug producers and dealers, American, Asian, and European. The situation in Afghanistan, the wars in Colombia between the various cartels, the fact that certain supply routes have run into problems in Russia, Albania, Iraq, and many other places, have created all kinds of difficulties. So it's become necessary to restore order and re-establish some kind of balance. Thus the need for a meeting at the very highest levels.'

He'd spoken with assurance and without interruption. The words had come from days and days of solitary reflection.

Pennisi looked at him in amazement.

'They'd said you were the best egg in the basket around here, but I had no idea . . . My compliments! You're right on the money!'

'How many participants will there be?'

'Twelve. We have the names. The biggest bosses of all. If you'd like to know . . .'

'No, I'm not interested. Do you know where and when they'll join the ship?'

'What questions! We know how to do our job, you know, and we do it pretty well. Two in Sfax, two in Piraeus, three in Malta, two in the Turkish part of Cyprus, two in Libya, and the last one will board from a trawler outside the port of Fiacca.'

Montalbano became curious. 'Is the last one Sicilian?'

'Yes. Paolino Contrera.'

'But aren't the Contreras in Canada?'

'That's true, but he's been back here for the past month. To take part in the summit, which has been long in preparation. And you know what? Almost none of these twelve men knows the others, except for the Bolivians. And this is an important detail.'

'Why?'

'Because, at the very last minute, while he's on the trawler, Paolino Contrera will be prevented from boarding the *Halcyon*. And someone else will take his place.'

'Who?'

'Me.'

Montalbano hesitated.

'But don't they know you?'

'Only by name. They know they've got Jack Pennisi on their tails and that he's worse than their shadows, but they don't know what I look like, and they don't know what Contrera looks like, either. This evening I'm going to be getting a passport with his name on it and my picture.'

'I'm sorry, but could you tell me what you're going to do, once you're aboard the ship, completely alone?'

'Look, they made a rule. None of the twelve bosses, who are coming without bodyguards, can carry a weapon.

They'll be searched in person by the captain. Only two crew members will be armed, in case of need. I, on the other hand, will be armed.'

'With what?'

'Contrera suffers from asthma, which everybody knows. And so he never goes anywhere without his inhaler. I've been given a special one, a bit bigger than the normal ones. It's full of knockout gas that takes immediate effect. Thirty seconds with the portholes closed is enough. I'll put it beside me on the table, within reach, and then at the right moment I'll open it. It makes no noise at all. And as soon as they're all asleep—'

'But will one canister be enough?'

'Each normal canister contains enough for two hundred hits, what's the right word . . .'

'Inhalations.'

'Well, in the one they've made for me, which, as I said, is a little bigger, the gas is super-compressed.'

'And what will you do after everyone passes out?'

'I'll go outside. I'll have about an hour to do what I need to do. I'll eliminate one of the guards, take his weapon, and then report the situation to you by radiophone.'

'To me?!'

'To you.'

'And mind telling me where I'll be?'

'You'll be onboard a trawler in the general area with three of your men. The fewer the better. Nobody must know anything. These twelve traffickers must disappear off the map.'

'I'm sorry, but who will relay your daily position to me on the trawler?'

'The *Halcyon* will be under surveillance day and night, once by helicopter, another time by a passing ship, another time by an aeroplane . . . All organized to perfection, have no fear.'

'And who's doing the music?'

Pennisi seemed not to have heard correctly. 'What did you say?'

'Who's writing the music?'

'What music?'

'The soundtrack for the film.'

Pennisi looked more and more confused. 'What film?'

'The James Bond film you just told me the plot of. You see, when I arrive with the trawler, it will be as if the Seventh Cavalry is coming, and we'll need a good epic soundtrack.'

'But this is not a movie! It's my plan for—'

'I'm sorry, I mistook it for a film.'

Only then did Pennisi begin to understand. He sat there for a moment in silence, then he began to frown.

'Are you mocking me?'

'A little,' Montalbano admitted.

'Why?'

'Because it would take only the slightest thing, a puff of wind, a spider's web, to throw your plan to the dogs.'

'Such as?'

'Such as a porthole not closing all the way, or somebody not wanting to close it, and all your gas is useless. Anyway, while you're eliminating one guard, who's to say the other won't sound the alarm?'

'Well, I must say in all modesty that I'm pretty good at this kind of thing. I don't make mistakes.'

'I don't doubt it. Still, it seems risky to me. This is a huge, unique opportunity, too big to jeopardize.'

Maybe the American had some doubts himself as to his own plan, because he immediately asked, 'Do you have any suggestions?'

'I'll have to think about that. Meanwhile, tell me: where is Zaccaria?'

'I've got Zaccaria. In a safe place, under continuous surveillance. He's waiting for a call from the captain of the *Halcyon,* who'll tell him when they're going to berth at Fiacca. That way Zaccaria has the time to go into town and order the supplies they need with two days' advance. Zaccaria is collaborating with us.'

'Is it true that this is the first time the *Halcyon* is calling at the port of Fiacca?'

'Yes.'

'The last time they were here in Vigàta, there were two sailors who disembarked to go and get the food and drink. Will it be the same men?'

'I don't know.'

'Could you ask Zaccaria?'

'Wait a second.'

He pulled out his mobile, dialled a number, and said something in American. Then he turned it off and put it back in his pocket.

'The shopping is always done by the ship's cook and his helper.'

A hint of an idea began to materialize in the inspector's brain. But he decided not to mention it to Pennisi. It was too early yet.

The American then looked at his watch. It was six p.m.

He sighed.

'Sorry, but I gotta go. Wanna take me to my car?'

'Are you busy now?'

'No, I just have to wait for the captain to phone Zaccaria.'

'Can't you wait here?'

'Sure, but I don't want to be a bother.'

'No bother at all! Do you like to walk?'

'I jog for an hour a day.'

'Then listen to me. We're going to take a walk along the beach as far as the Scala dei Turchi, from where you'll have a beautiful view of the sunset, then we'll come back home and have dinner together.'

The American answered with a blissful smile. 'OK,' he said. 'But before we go I need to use the *beccaus*.'

Montalbano didn't know what to say. Pennisi's Americanized Sicilian was sometimes incomprehensible to him. Pennisi noticed.

'You know, the facilities, the toilet.'

Sighing with relief, the inspector showed him the way.

*

As they strolled along the beach, Pennisi told him about his family and the chain of food shops his younger brothers owned. He himself had gone to university and become a lawyer, but he'd wanted to join the FBI because he had the mind of a policeman.

As they were watching the sunset while sitting on the white marl of the Scala dei Turchi, Montalbano felt curious about something.

'Why didn't you turn to the Narcotics division of the Italian police?'

Pennisi answered at once.

'Because there are close connections between half the world's Narcotics units. They're constantly exchanging intelligence . . . I was worried that someone might let slip, even accidentally, what I was doing here . . . And if that happened, goodbye, *Halcyon*!'

'So why did you choose me of all people?'

'We did some research. You're good, and you're a lone wolf.'

*

Later, Pennisi was in seventh heaven eating Adelina's *pasta 'ncasciata* out on the veranda with Montalbano.

'Did you make it yourself?'

'No, my housekeeper did. But in a pinch, I could make it myself.'

'Really?' said Pennisi, amazed.

'Sure. Theoretically speaking, I would be able, counting first and second courses, to cook ten or so decent dishes.'

After they'd finished the second course, a phone rang. It was Pennisi's. He listened for a few moments, then got up and went down to the beach. The inspector cleared the table and replaced the dishes and silverware with whisky, glasses, and ice cubes. Pennisi returned from the beach, sat down, and poured himself some whisky.

'There's news. Zaccaria got his call. The *Halcyon* will berth at Fiacca the day after tomorrow at five p.m. The shopping should be ready by six o'clock. The cook has told him what he needs. And at eight p.m. sharp they'll be putting out again. I told my man who's with Zaccaria to drive him to Fiacca tomorrow morning to do his shopping. He'll be calling me back in a minute to tell me the name of the trawler that Contrera will be boarding.'

'You're well organized, eh?'

'In all modesty, yes. And seeing that you've been unable to come up with any better ideas, I'll take that to mean we'll do as I said. You'll receive your instructions from the commissioner.'

'Actually, I do have a suggestion.'

'Then let's hear it, 'cause I have stuff to do and you have to give me a lift back to my car in a hurry.'

'You, in Fiacca, have to get the cook and his helper out of my way, however you can.'

'That's not a problem,' said Pennisi. 'But why?'

One unlikely American plot turn deserved another, thought Montalbano.

So he fired away: 'Because I and my assistant, Fazio, will be boarding in their place.'

The surprise made Pennisi's mask fall off. He poured himself half a glass of whisky and drank it neat.

'But who will give your names to the captain of the *Halcyon* as replacements for the two men I will have removed?'

'Easy: Zaccaria.'

FOURTEEN

'Explain.'

'Tomorrow, Zaccaria will be going to Fiacca to do the shopping. You told me so yourself. Which shops will he go to? Naturally, he'll go to a grocer, to a butcher for meat, to a fishmonger for fish to put in the freezer on board. You follow?'

'Sure.'

'But the grocer he goes to will have to be a bit out of the way.'

'Why?'

'Because five minutes before the *Halcyon* guys come to pick up the stuff, the police will replace the real salesman, or owner, or whatever he is, with a fake one, who will be an officer of mine, Catarella.'

'Why?' Pennisi asked again.

'Catarella will have already been equipped with a bag of salt or sugar that instead of being real salt or sugar will actually be a powerful sedative powder. Tell the commissioner to prepare this and give it to Catarella. The package will have to be recognizable, however – it could, for example, be the only packet of salt of a different brand from the rest. You should make them all the same but one. Clear?'

'Go on.'

'I happened to notice that the cook of the *Halcyon* and his helper seem normally to take a taxi to go and pick up the purchases, which are considerable in quantity. But how do they catch this taxi? Either they call for one by telephone and have it drive up to the ship's gangway on the quay, or else they go themselves to the taxi stand in the port. In either case, that will be the moment to take them out of circulation, and that's when you and your men come in. But it's important that it happens before everyone's eyes. Either they get hit by a car on their way to the taxi stand, or else, when coming off the ship to get in the taxi they've called, there'll be four drunks on the quay wanting the same cab, who'll start a brawl. A police car that will happen to be in the area at the time will then arrest everyone. At this point the captain will be forced to go to the police station to obtain the two men's release, where he'll be told that the men have been charged with resisting arrest, and that it'll be days before they can be set free. The captain won't be able to wait for them, since he has a tight schedule to keep. And so he calls Zaccaria for help. Who will tell him that he should try talking to Giuseppe Concordia.'

'And who's that?'

'A friend of his who's a cook by trade but is temporarily

on leave from the restaurant where he works. But in fact it'll be me.'

'So why is that his name?'

'*Matre santa,* Jack! It's just a random name I pulled out of a hat. If you don't like it you can choose another to put on the fake passport you have to have made for me within twenty-four hours. And you'll have to have another one ready for Fazio, too. This cook will play hard to get with Zaccaria. He'll ask for a lot of money, then will finally come around, after which he'll go and pick up the shopping in the company of his assistant, and together they'll board the ship.'

'And what happens next?'

'What happens next is that there'll be three of us onboard the *Halcyon.* It's better than you being there all by yourself, don't you think?'

'Yeah.'

'Then, when you give me the word, I'll take the sleeping powder and put it both in the bosses' food and in the crew's. After they're all fast asleep, we'll call another of my men, Augello, who'll be on the trawler navigating nearby, and we'll handcuff them all. What do you say?'

The American didn't waste any time.

His first gesture was a big, sudden clap on Montalbano's back that nearly made him cough up everything he'd just eaten. Then he said: 'I have to say, that's a really good plan you came up with. OK, we'll do as you say. But now take me to my car because I've really got a lot to do.'

On their way to Vigàta, they decided that the inspector

would wait to be called by the commissioner, who would explain to him exactly how to proceed.

'See you again on board! *In bocc'al lupo!*' said the American, shaking his hand before getting into the car.

'*Crepi*,' said Montalbano.

He waited for Pennisi to drive off, then blew on his fingers. Pennisi had practically fractured them.

*

Back home, he sat a long time on the veranda thinking carefully about what to tell Livia. He had to come up with a big lie to justify the fact that he would be away from home for several days and unable to call her.

In the end he concocted what he thought was a passable story. But he didn't want to waste any time, lest he forget it at once, and so he called her right away.

'Did you know I was unwell yesterday?'

'Oh, my God, what was it?'

'Dizziness, weakness . . . I had a bad night.'

'Did you see a doctor?'

'Yes, I went this morning. My blood pressure is very high. He gave me some pills, advised me to rest and take things calmly . . . But how am I supposed to stay calm in the midst of a veritable war with the commissioner?'

'You should get away from Vigàta, at least for a few days. Come back here.'

Montalbano pretended not to have heard that last statement.

'But you know what? At Enzo's today I met my lawyer,

the one who submitted my petition, and he was in the company of a friend of his who'd stopped by here with his boat, on his way to Malta. You won't believe it, but he invited me to come with him.'

'And what did you say to him?'

'Well, just like that, on the fly, with someone I don't really know . . .'

'Will you be seeing him again?'

'Tomorrow morning.'

'Tell him yes.'

'You think I should?'

'Of course! What better opportunity . . . How long will you be away?'

'About a week.'

'You'll feel so much better! You'll see. But don't forget to take your mobile.'

'Come on, like I'm going to forget something like that . . .'

And that was the last lie he told Livia.

*

He went to bed with his head free of worries.

How he should act once aboard the *Halcyon* was something he didn't really feel like thinking about at the moment. *To each day its suffering, to each hour its problem*, the aunt who raised him used to say.

*

The following morning, as soon as he awoke, feeling rested and refreshed, he packed a suitcase with enough stuff to stay away for a week or so. Then he felt overcome with doubt. Do ship's cooks bring their own aprons and chef's hats with them? If so, he'd better get hold of a cook's outfit over the course of the day. The apron he could probably find in a supermarket, but the hat? Too complicated. He decided to drop the whole idea. If anyone on the *Halcyon* asked him any questions, he would answer that his work clothes were at the cleaner's.

When Adelina arrived, he told her about half of the lie he'd told Livia; to wit, that he was going on a sailing trip with a friend.

'Should I cook a somathin' fer this evenin'?'

'For this evening, yes.'

At around eleven that morning the estate agency phoned. The usual girl wanted to inform him that Mr Bonifacio had called to say that he'd decided not to buy the house. Montalbano took advantage of the opportunity to tell her he would be out of town for about ten days.

He was on his way to have lunch at Enzo's, having already opened the door, when the telephone rang like sudden death.

'Montalbano?'

'Yes, Mr Commissioner.'

'I'm sending someone for you at four this afternoon, using the same method as before. Be sure to be ready.'

Of course he would be ready. At this point he was ready to take orders from anyone: the police, the FBI . . . Scotland Yard?

✲

'Want some *pasta alla carrittera*?'

'Sure, but then you have to give me the recipe.'

'Inspector, the recipe is only useful to those who know how to work a stove.'

'Don't you worry about that.'

'You want to get Adelina to make it?'

'Right.'

Enzo explained what to do, and Montalbano took a few notes. It was best for him to know as many things as possible about the art of cookery.

'And for the main course, would you like some swordfish *involtini*?'

'Yes, but you have to give the recipe for the *involtini* as well.'

'What is this? Do you want to open a trattoria and steal my customers?'

After eating, he walked along the jetty and sat down on the flat rock under the lighthouse.

He stayed there an hour, smoking one cigarette after another.

The moment he'd set foot outside the trattoria, he'd fallen into the grip of total panic.

Yes, panic. There was no other word for it.

What the hell was he thinking by proposing such an insane plan to the American?

Couldn't he just have kept his mouth shut?

It had to have been because he felt indirectly challenged by Pennisi. By his calm, his courage, the simplicity of the words he'd used to describe putting himself in mortal danger.

The inspector had wanted to seem on the same level and had upped the ante, as in a poker game.

But here the stakes weren't money, but their own lives.

Would he be up to the task, with all the weight of his years on his shoulders? He had serious doubts.

He felt that his reaction time was too slow at this stage of life, when a situation like this called for lightning-quick reflexes.

What had got into him?

But it was too late to turn back now.

He got up from the rock and looked around.

Would he ever see this landscape so dear to him again? '*Farewell, lighthouse rising from the waters and into the sky . . .*' he murmured.

*

At four o'clock sharp the usual policeman came to pick him up with the police van. Montalbano went through the same rigamarole as before, then found himself alone again in the small sitting room on the top floor of Montelusa Central.

A few minutes later Bonetti-Alderighi came in, all smiles.

'Pennisi told me everything. Your plan is brilliant. My compliments. We've made a really good impression on the FBI.'

Brilliant, my arse. And what was with the commissioner's 'we', anyway? Maybe before talking about good impressions, it might be better to wait and see how the whole thing turned out.

'Thanks.'

'Pennisi would like to play it a little more safely, however.'

'In what sense?'

'He wants your appearance to be sort of transformed. He's afraid that someone on board may have caught a glimpse of you when the *Halcyon* called at the port of Vigàta.'

'I don't understand.'

'You will soon enough. Do you know Santonastaso?'

'No. Who's he?'

'A magician. Just wait and you'll see. Afterwards, Santonastaso will take a few photographs.'

The inspector began to get worried. Magician, photographs . . .

'Would you please explain?'

'But it's obvious, Montalbano. The photos are for your passport. Speaking of which, your name will be . . . what was that? . . . ah, yes, Giuseppe Concordia.'

'May I?' a well-dressed man of about forty in civvies asked from the doorway. He smelled like a barber from a good ten yards away.

'Ah, here he is, our Santonastaso,' said the commissioner, rising to his feet. 'Trust him, Montalbano. You're in excellent hands. I'll be back in about an hour.'

Santonastaso put a briefcase on the floor, sat down opposite the inspector, and started looking at him without saying anything. Montalbano began to feel embarrassed and didn't know where to rest his eyes. A moment later, he didn't know where to rest his hands.

Then Santonastaso bent down in front of him and asked:

'May I?'

'Go ahead.'

He reached out, took the inspector's chin between thumb and forefinger, and turned his head to the left.

'Please stay that way.'

Moments later he turned the inspector's head to the right. 'Just be a little patient.'

Montalbano's balls started to spin. What was he, some kind of fashion model? Was this guy going to paint his portrait or something?

All at once a frightening thought occurred to him. What if this Santowhatshisname was a plastic surgeon? And wanted to operate on his face? What, were they kidding? He wasn't going to take this lying down. He would put the entire commissioner's building to fire and sword! But he managed, albeit with some effort, to restrain himself, waiting to see how things played out.

At last the magician spoke:

'Listen, I've decided to make your hair greyish-blond, given your age.'

On the one hand, the inspector was pleased to hear this; the guy was not a plastic surgeon but some kind of barber.

But on the other, he felt outraged – he could practically have shot him for those last words.

'But the moustache has definitely got to go.'

At this point Montalbano snapped: 'Out of the question!'

'But you see . . .'

'I said it's out of the question! And don't insist!'

Santonastaso got scared.

'As you wish, sir, but please calm down . . . Surely you'll allow me at least . . . to cut it a bit differently.'

'All right,' the inspector consented through clenched teeth.

'So shall we go into the bathroom?' said Santonastaso, picking up the briefcase.

*

The ordeal Santonastaso subjected him to lasted over an hour.

Head in the sink under the open tap, shampoo. 'Keep your eyes closed.'

Long blow-dry session. Head back in the sink, massaged and rubbed ad infinitum with some kind of liquid.

'Keep your eyes closed.'

Again the blow-dryer. Then there was a variation on the command: 'Throw your head back, but still keep your eyes closed.'

Santonastaso then got to work on his moustache. He clipped, combed, and then, after some scissor swishes, came more washings, rubbings, blow-dryings.

When not giving orders, the magician sang passages from Verdi's *Aida*, sometimes in a contralto voice, sometimes soprano.

Montalbano, on the other hand, was endlessly cursing the saints, not stopping for one second, but always keeping a religious silence, if the adjective can be properly applied to an uninterrupted, hour-long stream of blasphemies.

'OK, you can look now,' said Santonastaso, freeing him from the two towels in which he'd wrapped his head.

Upon opening his eyes, Montalbano very nearly had a heart attack. He almost fell out of his chair.

He was looking at the face of a first-class idiot with a British-style moustache. It wasn't his face. It did not belong to him.

The ash-blond hair made him look like a cross between an ageing male prostitute now out of commission and a former butler from some noble house. But more the first than the second, and it was possible that aboard the *Halcyon* some long-famished sailor might proposition him.

He looked simply pukeworthy.

'What do you think?' the magician asked proudly.

The inspector didn't have time to tell him what he thought, and a good thing, too, because the commissioner suddenly appeared and said: 'That's extraordinary! Bravo, Santonastaso!'

The magician bowed as if onstage. 'However . . .' the commissioner began.

Santonastaso froze like a wind-up doll whose spring had jammed.

'However?' Montalbano asked in a faint voice.

What new ordeals did these guys want to put him through?

'Just one final touch, and the transformation would be

perfect. But that final touch is still lacking,' the commissioner concluded.

'Wait,' said the magician.

He bent down, riffled through his briefcase, and extracted two pairs of glasses.

He examined them, chose a pair of wire rims, and put them on Montalbano. Who resumed his silent litany of curses.

The lenses were not corrective, but it was the very idea of glasses that so distressed and angered him.

He didn't even have the courage to look at himself in the mirror.

'Perfect!' the commissioner rejoiced. 'OK, now let's go into the other room and take the photos. We haven't any time to waste.'

*

After Santonastaso had left, the commissioner went over to the sitting-room door and locked it. Montalbano took advantage of the moment to remove his glasses.

'No no no! Put them back on! You have to get used to them!'

The inspector put them back on. The commissioner then pulled out a phone and handed it to him.

'At the moment only Pennisi and I know the number of this phone. Later I'll give it to Fazio, and Pennisi will tell it to Zaccaria. Nobody else will have it. Do not bring it with you onboard the *Halcyon*. We've put the numbers that might be useful to you in the memory.'

'Where should I leave it?'

'In the little flat in Fiacca.'

'I have a little flat in Fiacca?'

'Yes, as of this morning. At Via Bixio, 32. Take this down, please.'

The inspector obeyed. After dictating Fazio's number to him as well, the commissioner continued: 'It's a small house, two floors. A little old lady lives on the ground floor, alone. It's a bit on the outskirts, but just a few steps outside the door there's a bus stop from where you can go straight into town.'

'When do I go to Fiacca?'

'At ten-thirty this evening a taxi will come up to your door. Don't worry, the apartment is in perfect order and can be moved into at once. We've already used it on other occasions. And the fridge is full. But you can eat out, if you prefer. Someone will call on you around eight o'clock tomorrow morning and bring you your passport. At eleven o'clock you must go to the cafe-gelateria located on the left-hand side of the large piazza by the sea and stand with your back to the buildings. After a while Zaccaria will appear, you'll greet each other like old friends, and you will pretend to give him your mobile number. And if there are people around, make it so they can hear what you're saying. You're a professional chef from a famous Milanese restaurant that's temporarily closed for renovations. You've taken advantage of the break to come to the famous Fiacca hot springs for your rheumatism, and you've been there before. It was a relative of your assistant who found you the little flat, and this assistant has come along with you to Sicily. Speaking of which, we've given Fazio the name of Angelo Verruso, which will be on his passport. All clear?'

'Perfectly.'

'That's all I have to tell you. Everything else will be up to you.'

Bonetti-Alderighi stood up and opened his arms.

'Good luck.'

Montalbano mistook the commissioner's gesture as one of resignation, like throwing up his hands, as if he were saying that from this point on one could do nothing, that there was no turning back or changing one's already assigned fate, and so the inspector threw up his hands himself and gave a slight shrug of the shoulders.

But that was not the commissioner's intention. In fact he took two steps forward and embraced Montalbano. Then he left.

Feeling weak in the knees, the inspector collapsed into a chair.

If Bonetti-Alderighi wanted to embrace him, it was a sure sign that this was a mission of no return.

The policeman waiting for him outside the lift set his eyes on him and then looked away. He hadn't recognized him.

'It's me,' said Montalbano.

'I'm sorry,' said the policeman, opening the door of the van.

*

He couldn't eat on the veranda. He was afraid someone might see him and call the police, saying there was a stranger in Montalbano's house.

He ate in the kitchen, slowly, savouring every nuance of flavour, a bit like a condemned man having his last meal.

He then closed the windows and shutters, and at ten thirty sharp he heard a horn outside his door.

So he picked up his suitcase and left.

FIFTEEN

The apartment – bedroom, dining room, sitting room, bathroom, and kitchen – was pleasant, comfortable, and clean. There was even a dishwasher and a television. The woman on the ground floor hadn't seen him enter; at that hour she must have been already in bed.

He went into the bathroom and bristled the moment he saw his face in the mirror. In the car on the way there, lost in thought about what awaited him in the coming days, he'd completely forgotten about his new look.

He realized it would be hard for him to shave the following morning. He disliked himself too much, couldn't stand himself, in fact. If nature had actually given him that face from the start, he certainly would never have become a police detective. Inspector Salvo Montalbano would never have existed.

Does a man's face determine his fate?

Somebody born with the face of a whore was unlikely to be canonized a saint. Though there were exceptions.

But why had Pennisi had the brilliant idea to reduce him

to such a state? The commissioner had given only a partial explanation. The more he thought about it, however, the more he became convinced the fault was entirely his own. He had no one to blame but himself. If he'd only remained silent when the American was revealing his plan, if only he hadn't let himself get carried away by his desire to compete with Pennisi. The guy would have been perfectly content with the play-acting of his fake dismissal and the dispersal of his team. And nobody would ever have dreamt of any joint effort between Montalbano and some FBI agents.

But since the plans had changed and, thanks to his brilliant idea, he was now required to participate, poisson-ally in poisson, in the operation, to the point of having to board the *Halcyon* as the cook, Pennisi wanted to be absolutely certain that no one would recognize him.

Instead of getting angry at him, he should have thanked him. Pennisi did what he did for the success of the mission, of course, but also for the inspector's personal safety.

*

He finally fell asleep in the early morning, after thrashing about endlessly trying to get used to the new bed.

When he was woken up by the intercom buzzer, it was already broad daylight outside. He looked at his watch. Eight o'clock.

'Who is it?'

'Postman.'

Naked but for his underpants, he pushed the button and opened the door.

A postman in civvies but wearing the cap to his uniform appeared, bag full of letters, magazines, and newspapers.

'This is for you,' he said, handing him a yellow envelope.

'Thank you,' said the inspector.

It was addressed to Mr Giuseppe Concordia, Via Bixio, 32, Fiacca. It was even stamped, but Montalbano knew it was all fake, just like the postman himself. He opened the letter.

Inside was a passport, also fake, featuring a photo of his new face.

Which, now that it had been stamped, looked even worse than in the mirror.

In the kitchen he found the coffee and the espresso pot and made a cup. It came out well. Afterwards, shaving proved an ordeal, just as he'd foreseen.

The shower likewise, because Santowhatthefuck had advised that he not wash his hair, as the dye might start to fade before it was supposed to. He decided to buy himself a shower cap and take it onboard with him.

*

He went out shortly before ten o'clock and, already knowing the town well, went on foot to his appointment. On the way he stopped at a supermarket and bought a shower cap and soap.

It was a sunny day, and the cafe had put its tables out on the terrace. Most were already taken by people enjoying lemon ices. He'd just ordered one for himself when he heard a voice calling: 'Giuseppe! Giuseppe!'

He paid no attention, convinced they weren't calling him. Then the same voice, from a bit closer, cried: 'Concordia!'

Damn, he'd forgotten that was his name! He wasn't right in the head. And so, as an infiltrator, you couldn't really say he was off to a brilliant start.

He stood up and found himself in the arms of Zaccaria, who kissed him on both cheeks.

'Zaccaria!'

'Concordia!'

They hugged again, like two old friends genuinely happy to see each other.

'Have a seat and get yourself a granita,' said Montalbano.

'With pleasure,' said Zaccaria, accepting the invitation.

Then, looking Montalbano in the eye, the bastard grinned and said: 'You know, I think you look really good this way.'

Was the guy putting him on?

The inspector didn't let the opportunity slip.

'You on the other hand look a bit the worse for wear. Too many worries?'

The other changed the subject. 'So, what brings you this way?'

As they were eating their ices, Montalbano, in a voice loud enough for people at the surrounding tables to hear, began telling him how his current employer, the restaurant in Milan, was temporarily closed at the moment, and so his assistant had found him a nice apartment down here for the duration. He would remain in Fiacca for a month or so, taking the cure at the baths.

At this point Zaccaria asked him for his mobile number. Montalbano gave him one off the top of his head; he must already have known the real one.

Zaccaria jotted it down on a piece of paper.

Then he looked at his watch and said: 'I'll give you a call tomorrow. But now I have to go, because—'

'I'll walk with you a little way,' said the inspector, interrupting him. 'I haven't got anything pressing to do, so I might as well,' he continued, leaving the money for the ices on the tray.

It was better if everyone in town saw them walking arm in arm like two old friends.

At that moment a well-dressed fortyish man seated with a young blonde at the table beside theirs stood up, came over to them, and asked Montalbano: 'Excuse me, I believe I heard you say you're a chef.'

The inspector looked in bewilderment at Zaccaria, who returned an even more bewildered glance.

'Yes, that's right.'

'May I sit down with you?'

'To be honest, we were just leaving.'

'I'll only keep you a few minutes. Forgive my curiosity, but what restaurant in Milan are you a chef at?'

'. . . At the Don Lisander.'

He'd been there once and eaten well. Who knew whether it even still existed. The stranger looked at him in admiration.

'My name is Antonio Butera,' he said.

'Pleased to meet you. Giuseppe Concordia.'

The man didn't so much as cast a glance at Zaccaria. 'I'll get straight to the point. In ten days I'll be opening a restaurant near the baths. A really fancy one. I've been putting a lot of ads in the papers and on TV. Would you like to be my chef?'

'Haven't you got one already?'

'Yes, but I don't think he's on your level. And so far I haven't found anyone better.'

'But, my good man, I have no intention of leaving the Don Lisander.'

'I understand. But I'm asking you to be my chef only for as long as you'll be in Fiacca. That sort of thing is very important in launching a new restaurant, you know. I would pay you very well.'

Montalbano felt quite confused.

Was the story this man was telling him true or false? Was this Butera's name really Butera, or was he one of Pennisi's men? And if he was, what could this little intrusion mean? Maybe it was best to play for time.

'Look, I can't promise you anything, but I'll think about it. Give me a call in two or three days.'

'All right. Could you give me your mobile number?'

Montalbano dictated another number off the top of his head. Then he stood up and gestured to Zaccaria to do the same, and the two walked away from the cafe together.

Once they were out of range, the inspector asked: 'Did you order the shopping?'

'Yes.'

'Give me the grocer's address.'

'There's no need. I'll be taking you there myself.'

*

At around half-past twelve, as he was heading back to the apartment on foot, his phone rang. It was Fazio.

'Should we be meeting?'

'Don't you think it's better if we meet later, after I call you to suggest that you come along with me on the *Halcyon*?' said the inspector.

'Chief, I think it's better if we meet before, believe me. I have a good excuse: I can come by your place now to find out how you like it.'

'OK. I'll be waiting.'

*

Once he got home, he decided to practise. The fridge and cupboard were full of everything imaginable. Menu: *spaghetti alla chitarra* and fillet in wine.

No, too complicated. The fillet would have to be thawed, and to cook it in wine would take too long. He decided to thaw two steaks and put a pan of water on the stove. There were many kinds of pasta, but he couldn't find any *spaghetti alla chitarra,* and so decided that a dish of regular *spaghetti all'aglio e olio* would do fine.

But how would a chef from the Don Lisander actually practise? Who was he trying to kid? He heard the intercom buzzer ring.

'Who is it?'

'Verruso.'

Who was that? Then, luckily, he remembered that that was Fazio's new name.

No, this whole business was not for him. Not a good thing. Too old, he no longer had a memory, he told himself in dismay.

He opened the door and his jaw dropped.

The man standing before him had completely white, very curly hair and a close-cropped beard, also white. He also had a strange mouth that transformed his face: the lips were too prominent and partially exposed his teeth.

'What did they do to you?' Fazio asked.

'Why, haven't you looked in the mirror yourself?' Montalbano retorted. Then he asked: 'How long's your hairdo supposed to last? And what did they do to your lips?'

'The hairdo should last about a week. As for the lips, that bastard Santonastaso gave me two injections.'

'Maybe it'd be better,' said the inspector, 'if I phoned Zito and asked him to film us auditioning as a comedy team.'

While they were eating, Fazio reported that the commissioner's office had made him take a crash course in nautical and aeronautical signals, which included, just to be safe, some rudimentary instructions on how a ship's kitchen functioned. Montalbano felt mildly relieved.

They'd finished and were having coffee when Pennisi rang.

'How are you doing?'

'Fine.'

'The *Halcyon* just phoned Zaccaria. They'll be in the haba at five.'

Haba? What was that? From babas to habas? 'I'm sorry, but what's a *haba*?'

'You know . . . the port.'

'Ah, the harbour. And what am I supposed to do?'

'If all goes well, Zaccaria will come and get you between six and seven o'clock. So it's best if you stay at home. Give Fazio a ring and tell him to remain on hand. Bye-bye.'

Montalbano told Fazio everything Pennisi had just said.

Then they started talking about Trincanato's murder, and Fazio confessed that he felt uneasy knowing their lives were in the hands of a killer like Zaccaria. How could anyone trust a man like that?

Montalbano reassured him, pointing out that Zaccaria was in turn dependent upon Pennisi, who must have scared him out of his wits. Zaccaria was well aware that Pennisi wouldn't think twice before killing him if he made one false move.

The inspector then remembered something and wanted to tell Fazio.

'You know that time you came to my place after Trincanato's murder, the night there was a lunar eclipse? I forgot to tell you I saw the *Halcyon*.'

Fazio looked at him incredulously. 'Are you sure about that?'

'Absolutely.'

In a flash, Montalbano understood everything.

He'd fallen asleep in front of the television and had dreamt the eclipse. He'd dreamt his own destiny.

This had been happening for some time, starting with the dream in which he'd got married and a sailing ship had rammed them . . . Was this a good or a bad sign?

He found the strength to smile at Fazio, who kept looking at him with concern.

'I'm sorry, you're right. I was confusing it with something else.'

*

Left to himself, just to pass the time he put on an apron and washed the dishes, cutlery, and glasses by hand. Afterwards he lay down in bed.

From that moment forward, he was running on alternating current, smoking one cigarette after another.

For the first half-hour he felt calm, serene, and maybe even a little happy.

His imminent journey aboard the *Halcyon* was beginning to seem to him like a kind of cruise, a carefree holiday in the open air with the splashing of the sea and the flapping of the sails as continuous background music, and the scent of the brine regaling his senses . . . A dream come true.

In the half-hour that followed, the scene changed.

There was a storm at sea, he found himself barricaded in the *Halcyon*'s kitchen as the crew tried to break down the door, dressed like Malay pirates, one with a wooden leg, another a spitting image of Captain Hook, another with a black patch over one eye . . . A nightmare.

By six o'clock he couldn't take it anymore. He was drenched in sweat, so he got up and took a shower.

As he was coming out, the mobile rang.

'The cook and his helper have been arrested. It's your move now,' said Pennisi.

And he hung up.

It was as if he'd pressed his foot on the accelerator of Montalbano's heart. How fast was it going? A hundred and fifty kilometres an hour? He'd noticed a bottle of whisky. He poured himself half a glass, neat, and started sipping it slowly. He started sweating again. At ten minutes to seven the mobile made its presence known.

'Zaccaria here. Where are you?'

'At home. Why?'

'I need to talk to you about something important. I'm coming over with a friend. Make sure you're alone.'

'OK.'

The game had begun.

But who was this friend coming over with Zaccaria? That was not in the script.

*

Zaccaria seemed nervous. The man with him was a tall, well-dressed forty-year-old with black hair, moustache, and grey eyes as cold as the polar ice caps. Zaccaria introduced him as Juan Bartocelli, an Argentinian of Italian parents who spoke Italian well.

Bartocelli spoke first.

'I apologize, Mr Concordia, if I seem hurried, but I really don't have much time. I'm in charge of organizing the cruises of the *Halcyon*, which is a large schooner. These are rather unusual cruises, in that they're exclusive meetings among very high-level businessmen, financial gatherings that must remain unknown to the press, that sort of thing. Just a short while ago our cook and his assistant, who'd gone ashore to get provisions, were arrested over a silly quarrel. We can't afford to wait for them to be released, and so we'll have to replace them. My friend Zaccaria here mentioned your name to me and explained why, luckily for us, you're temporarily here in Fiacca. So, to get to the point: would you be willing to come aboard the *Halcyon* and be our chef?'

'Thanks, but no.'

'Why not?'

'Because, as I'm sure Zaccaria told you, I'm here in Fiacca to take the cure, but above all to rest.'

'But you'll be able to rest aboard the *Halcyon* just the same! You can bring your assistant along, if you like. He can prepare everyone's breakfast so that you can sleep as late as you like and go out and enjoy the sun on the deck. Anyway, we're not of course a restaurant with a continual influx of customers. We are what we are, and there are eighteen of us. And we're all on the same schedule: lunch at one p.m. and dinner at eight. It shouldn't be too much work for you.'

'That's what you think.'

'At any rate, it wouldn't be for very long.'

'No?'

'No. Six days, no more. And so, once the cruise was over, you'd still have three weeks left to take your cure. We set sail in an hour, at eight o'clock.'

Montalbano made a thoughtful face and said nothing.

'On top of everything else, you'll be paid better than you can possibly imagine,' Bartocelli added, throwing down his ace.

'How much?'

'Let's say twenty thousand per day for you, and three thousand for your assistant.'

'Let's make it two hundred thousand in all. I'll take care of my assistant myself. But I'll want an advance.'

'All right. Is fifty thousand OK?' Bartocelli said at once.

'It's fine.'

The younger man held out his hand. Shaking it, Montalbano felt as if he'd touched the cold skin of a snake.

'I'm going to go back to the ship on foot,' said Bartocelli. 'I'll leave the taxi here to wait for you. Zaccaria will stay with you. Please call your assistant and pack as quickly as you can. Zaccaria will tell you where to pick up the shopping, which has already been ordered.'

As he left he cast a glance of understanding at the other.

'Watch out for this Bartocelli when you're on board, sir,' said Zaccaria, after the man had left. 'This is the first time I'm seeing him, but even the captain seems to take orders from him. And Pennisi never mentioned him to me; he himself may not even know he's onboard the ship.'

✡

He arranged to meet Fazio outside the grocer's on Via Pusateri. Then, since there was so much stuff to pick up, Zaccaria called another taxi to load the meat and fish and take it directly to the ship.

When the inspector got there, Fazio was already waiting outside the shop with a suitcase in his hand. They put it on the roof of the car, next to his own.

Meanwhile, an elderly lady went into the shop. They followed her.

Catarella, wearing an apron, was behind the counter. 'Whaddya like?' he asked the woman.

The granny looked at him with suspicion. 'Isn't Don Totò here?'

'No, signora, 'e ain't feelin' so good.'

'But whenever he's not here, his wife takes his place!' the woman said.

'She's ill, too.'

Catarella was managing pretty well.

'And who are you?'

What a pain in the arse! 'I'm their nephew.'

'How come I've never seen you before?'

''Cause I woik in Joimany.'

'All right, give me a hundred grams of provolone.'

'Sweet or sharp?'

'Sharp.'

Montalbano and Fazio watched him in admiration as he cut, weighed, and wrapped the cheese, then took the woman's money and gave her the change. Then it was their turn.

'An' wha' wou' the jinnilmen like?' He hadn't recognized them.

So much the better. Apparently Santonastaso had done a good job.

'Zaccaria brought the list,' said Montalbano.

Catarella recognized the inspector by his voice, and the effect on him was unsettling. His eyes bulged out, then he paled, then blushed, then started slowly bending at the knees, and finally disappeared behind the counter.

'*Matre santa!*' said Fazio. 'He fainted!'

But Catarella was already slowly reappearing, bracing himself against the counter with both his hands.

'Ch . . . Ch . . . Chief . . .'

'Cool it, Cat!' Montalbano ordered him.

'I beck yer partin and unnastandin', Chief, bu' I got took a li'l by surprise. Iss all ready.'

'Help us load the stuff into the taxi.'

SIXTEEN

As they were loading, the inspector noticed that seven salt packets were white and one was green. That must be the one with the sedative.

Immediately afterwards, however, Catarella arrived with eight packets of sugar, seven of which were red, and one yellow.

Montalbano was worried.

Grabbing Catarella by the arm, he asked him under his breath: 'Where's the sedative?'

'Where iss asposta be, Chief.'

'OK, but is it in the green bag of salt or the yellow bag of sugar?'

''Ey tol' me iss in witta green salt.'

'Sure about that?'

'Sure as deat', Chief.'

Moments later, however, Catarella came back looking mortified.

'I'm rilly rilly sorry, Chief, but I'm not so sure anymores.

Jess now I 'ad a 'ammalitic doubt, like you call it. An' I tought maybe 'ey said it was inna yellow sugar.'

Montalbano gave him a withering look. He could have killed him. He limited himself to cursing five or six saints. But nastily.

*

At the foot of the gangway the usual sailor was standing guard, but this time there were two mates of his waiting for the taxi's arrival, to unload the provisions.

On board, right at the top of the gangway, were Zaccaria and Bartocelli, waiting for them.

'Have you got everything?' Montalbano asked Zaccaria from the quay as he got out of the taxi.

'Got it all.'

Laden with goods, Fazio introduced himself to Bartocelli, who shook his hand distractedly, then disappeared down a hatch.

Montalbano remained on the quay to make sure the taxi was empty, when he suddenly found Bartocelli next to him. 'Here's your advance,' he said, handing him an envelope. 'I'll pay the driver, and meanwhile you go onboard with Zaccaria, who will show you the galley and the pantry.'

*

After Montalbano climbed the gangway, Zaccaria told him to follow him.

To go belowdecks, the schooner had two hatches exactly

like those on the ferries. The wooden stairs were equipped with shiny, polished banisters.

'The *Halcyon* has two lower decks,' explained Zaccaria. 'The first one has all the cabins for the passengers and the captain and crew. The second, lower one has the big central salon, the crew's mess room afore, and, astern, the galley, pantry, cold-storage room, and the auxiliary engine room.'

They went down to the second deck. For each flight of stairs there was a landing with two doors giving onto it, which didn't have the usual small, sealed windows.

The galley was fairly large, the gas stove had six burners, and to the right and left of it were two metal cupboards, one with tablecloths and napkins, the other with cutlery, dishes, and glasses. There was even a dishwasher. The saucepans and frying pans were hanging over the sink. Beneath the sink was a small cabinet with four drawers full of knives, ladles, serving spoons, measuring cups, and carving forks. The kitchen was also endowed with a small table and two chairs, all screwed to the floor.

Next to the galley was the rather spacious cold-storage room, and beyond that was the pantry.

'So where do I sleep?' asked Montalbano.

'On the deck above this, with the crew.'

At that moment Fazio came in.

'I put your suitcase in a single cabin. Since there's not a full crew, there's room.'

Once they'd finished talking, Bartocelli appeared, flashing a hyenalike smile.

'Excuse me, this may come as something of a surprise,

but there are some very strict rules aboard the *Halcyon* that must be observed at all times. Transgressors will be subject to severe penalties. Do either of you have any weapons with you?'

Montalbano and Fazio put on their comedy-team act. First they looked at each other as if they'd never even heard that word pronounced before, then they looked simultaneously at Bartocelli and said in unison: 'Weapons?!'

'What about mobiles?' Bartocelli asked.

'I left mine in Fiacca,' said Montalbano. 'I guessed there wouldn't be any reception out on the open sea.'

'I was thinking the same thing,' said Fazio.

'Just let me check, so there won't be any problems, and that way we'll be better friends.'

'OK,' the Montalbano–Fazio duo said again in unison. He began to frisk them hastily, with professional precision. And he noticed that Montalbano was smiling. 'You find this amusing?'

'I'm ticklish.'

Bartocelli realized he was mocking him. At that moment his right hand was between Montalbano's legs and it sprang at once, grabbing his balls and squeezing just as much as was needed.

'You still need these, or shall I take them away?'

Now it was Bartocelli who was smiling. Montalbano made a worried face and said: 'I was smiling because I realized you were forgetting to look at our bags.'

Bartocelli let go and his smile broadened.

'I've already done that. Before coming down here.' His expression changed.

'We're already running quite late. Get dinner ready at once. Something quick. I suggest spaghetti with tuna, followed by steak.'

'For how many?'

'Four sailors, the captain, me, and you two.' Then, turning to Zaccaria: 'You come with me. I need to talk to you.'

As the two were leaving the kitchen, Montalbano wiped the sweat from his brow. If he hadn't answered him the right way, Bartocelli would have been quite capable of harming him severely.

They heard the auxiliary engines start up.

'Go and get a few small cans of tuna, some olive oil, and a bag of salt – a white bag, mind you – while I put the pasta water on the stove.'

As a cooking debut, you couldn't really say it was very challenging. Fazio returned with what he'd asked for. He looked bewildered.

'What's wrong?'

'Chief . . .'

'Don't call me that, not even when we're alone. Get used to it.'

'From the porthole in the pantry you can see the gangway above. It's been removed.'

'So?'

'But Zaccaria didn't have time to get off the ship!'

'Are you sure?'

'Absolutely!'

'But Bartocelli didn't count him among those who needed to eat. So he must have got off.'

'I don't know what to say.'

'Listen. For the moment we'll stop thinking about it. Get a knife and go into the cooler and cut eight steaks. Luckily the meat won't be frozen yet.'

With a certain thrilling sensation, Montalbano distinctly felt the *Halcyon* beginning to move.

Moments later the internal phone rang. It was Bartocelli.

'We'll all be eating in the crew mess. Verruso should come and lay the table for six.'

'Will I and my assistant also be joining you?'

'No, you two will eat in the kitchen.'

When Fazio returned with the steaks, Montalbano said to him: 'They want the table laid for six. Which confirms that Zaccaria had time to disembark.'

Fazio said nothing, but merely loaded everything onto a trolley and went out. He returned less than ten minutes later.

'We're already outside the harbour,' he said.

*

Montalbano had almost finished draining the spaghetti when the internal phone buzzed. It was Bartocelli again.

'Shall I send someone for the spaghetti?'

'Yes.'

Three sailors came in, took two dishes each, and went

back out without a word. Montalbano and Fazio ate at their little table without bothering to lay it.

The inspector noticed with satisfaction that his pasta was neither overdone nor too al dente. One ate it with pleasure.

They followed the same procedure for the second course as with the first.

'Apparently they don't want us to have any contact with the crew,' Fazio remarked.

'But it's inevitable that we will, sooner or later,' Montalbano observed.

'Of course, but not while eating, because people tend to talk at the table,' Fazio countered.

Afterwards, Bartocelli called again and ordered them to come and clear the table and clean up. Montalbano asked him if they wanted coffee, and he replied they would make it themselves with the coffee machine in the mess room.

Fazio grumbled that he'd agreed to come aboard as a chef's assistant, not as a waiter, but then he went out with the trolley, a broom, and a dustpan.

*

He returned fifteen minutes later, and the inspector noticed that he was rather glum.

'Something happen?'

'The moment I entered the mess, Bartocelli asked me in English if I spoke English.'

'And what did you say?'

'I pretended I didn't understand the question.'

'Then what?'

'Then Bartocelli said to the captain, in English, that in half an hour, as soon as they were far enough out to sea, they would have to make a decision about the man. And I'm sure they were talking about Zaccaria.'

Montalbano felt a high-voltage electrical charge run up his spine.

'*Matre santa!*' was all he managed to say, under his breath.

The temperature in the kitchen suddenly went up. Despite the two big running ventilators. Montalbano felt as if he couldn't breathe.

When, by an effort of will, he recovered slightly, he managed to continue.

'That's why they kept him aboard!'

'What did I tell you?'

'So they discovered that Zaccaria had betrayed them!'

'That's for sure,' said Fazio. 'But there are two questions. Do they also know who we are? And who informed them of the betrayal?'

Overcoming his initial fear, Montalbano managed, with some difficulty, to get his brain working again. A few seconds later he'd reached a conclusion and told Fazio. 'Off the top of my head, I don't think they know who we are.'

'Why do you say that?'

'Because by now we'd already be keeping Zaccaria company.'

'But what would they do without any cooks?'

'Oh, come on! For two or three days, they'd get by on bread and cheese, then they'd just bring on a replacement from somewhere else.'

'So who do you think ratted on Zaccaria?'

'But are we so sure he was ratted on? That they discovered he'd betrayed them?'

Fazio looked at him in astonishment.

'Why else would they want to get rid of him?'

'Because it was he who, with Fantuzzo's help, killed Trincanato, no? Fantuzzo was taken out by the Organized Crime Unit, and now they eliminate Zaccaria to burn all bridges between them and the murder. Or so they think. Because they don't know that Zaccaria has already confessed.'

'Oh!' exclaimed Fazio, not terribly convinced.

At that moment Bartocelli appeared.

'If you've finished here in the kitchen, I would ask you both to retire to your quarters and stay there. We're having a meeting on deck. Tomorrow morning you're to have breakfast ready for nine people by seven o'clock. And, I repeat, for now, no matter what happens, you're to remain in your quarters for the rest of the evening and not come out for any reason whatsoever. That's an order.'

And he turned around and headed up the stairs. Montalbano put out the light, closed the door, and followed Fazio, who was leading the way.

They went up to the deck above them. Fazio opened a door, and they found themselves looking down a corridor with cabins on both sides.

'These are for the passengers,' said Fazio.

He opened another door, which gave onto a landing with stairs going both up and down. In front was a third door. Beyond it, the crew's quarters.

Two cabins, a large room with four bunk beds, two bathrooms.

They didn't run across a living soul. Fazio opened the first cabin on the right. 'You'll sleep here,' he said.

'And what about you?'

'I'm in the big room with the crew.'

'Why's that?'

'It's what Bartocelli wants. But, all things considered, it's better this way, since I'll be able to hear what the men are saying.'

'Just stay here a minute while I put my stuff in order,' said Montalbano.

Once he'd finished emptying his suitcase, he noticed that Fazio had opened the porthole and was trying to work out what was going on on the upper deck.

'I can hear voices, but can't understand what they're saying.'

'Shall we go and see?' the inspector ventured.

'How would we do that?'

'There are two hatches, one afore and one astern. I just now noticed that the one closer to us, at the fore, is shut. We can go and check the other one at the stern.'

They went out of the cabin and all the way back up the corridor, at the end of which the inspector opened, ever so slightly, the door giving on to the landing from which the staircase led up to the stern hatch.

He closed it at once.

Fazio was glued to him from behind.

'On the top stair,' he said in a very soft voice, 'you can see a sailor's feet. Bartocelli must have posted him there as a guard.'

'So there's nothing we can do.'

'Let's just wait a little. Maybe he'll move.'

'Better keep an eye on him,' said Fazio, moving in front of Montalbano.

He reopened the door a crack and started watching. Montalbano heard the distant sound of raucous laughter.

Probably the only person who didn't find the joke funny was Zaccaria.

At that moment, he suddenly realized without a doubt that Bartocelli already had in his head, from the very moment he and Fazio had agreed to work on the ship, the intention of killing them both rather than letting them disembark when the cruise ended.

There was no way they could be allowed to live, having been witnesses of so important a summit.

Bartocelli was determined to make them meet the same end as Zaccaria.

'He's gone up,' said Fazio.

And he took a step aside to let Montalbano see for himself. It was true; the feet were gone.

'But he must still be somewhere very close by,' the inspector commented.

'I'll go and look,' Fazio said resolutely.

And before Montalbano could stop him, Fazio pushed him aside and went out.

The inspector re-closed the door, leaving it open just a tiny crack.

In a flash Fazio was standing on the first step. There were only two more to go before his eyes would be at the same level as the deck.

He went up them with his back to Montalbano, extremely deliberately, as if in slow motion. At the third step he froze, ready to dive back down and into the door that Montalbano was now holding open for him.

The inspector then saw Fazio's hand move, signalling to him to come and look for himself.

Montalbano repeated what he'd just seen Fazio do, and quickly found himself beside him.

The sailor on guard, submachine-gun slung over his shoulder, stood at least six strides away from the hatch and had his back to them, absorbed in the scene unfolding at the foot of the main mast, which was completely lit up by a floodlight.

They were hanging Zaccaria.

He was gagged, with hands and feet bound, and held upright by a sailor while a third man slipped the noose around his neck and a fourth held the end of the rope, which passed through one of the mast's blocks about ten feet off the deck, ready to pull on it.

It looked just like a scene from a movie about pirates, except that it was tragically real.

Despite the distance, Montalbano noticed that Zaccaria was trembling all over, as though an electrical current were running through him, and realized that the dark stain at the front of his trousers must have been piss.

Maybe that was what the sailors had been having such a laugh about.

Then Bartocelli, standing beside the captain, who was smoking his pipe, cool as a cucumber, gave an order.

The third sailor started pulling on the rope.

The remaining crew members started clapping their hands and laughing.

Zaccaria's body twisted and writhed in mid-air like a snake's. Then it stopped moving.

Bartocelli shouted another order.

The sailor holding the rope lowered the body until its feet touched the wood of the deck. Then Bartocelli spoke.

'What did he say?' the inspector asked in Fazio's ear. Fazio gestured that he hadn't understood.

But then, to their dismay, they saw two sailors pull out knives and start arguing.

They stopped only when Bartocelli barked an order. One of the two put his knife back into his pocket.

The other, who was the one who'd put the noose around Zaccaria's neck, then approached the dead body and in a single stroke slashed open the stomach with an upwards motion, from the groin all the way to the bottom of the rib cage.

The entrails, like snakes emerging from a pit, started slithering over the wooden deck.

Bartocelli said something, laughing.

'What did he say?'

'He said that this way, the fish'll do a better job eating him up.'

Montalbano couldn't take it and ran away.

He got to his cabin just in time to vomit in the sink.

Fazio came in right behind him. He was deathly pale. 'They threw the body into the sea and are now washing the blood off the deck. I'm going to go to bed, so that when they come in I can pretend I'm asleep.'

'I don't think they'll be coming down any time soon,' said Montalbano.

'Why do you say that?'

'Because in a little while they're going to meet the trawler.'

'What trawler?'

'The one bringing Contrera, the first participant in the summit.'

'But how do you know this?'

'Pennisi told me. And he also told me that he'll be coming in Contrera's place, since nobody's ever seen Contrera.'

*

Fifteen minutes later Montalbano, who'd already gone to bed, heard the *Halcyon*'s engines stop.

Then, in the sudden, deep silence, he could hear the sound of a diesel engine drawing near. It had to be Pennisi's trawler.

He was about to get up and look out of the porthole when he heard the faintest of sounds. He froze, keeping his eyes shut but leaving a tiny crack to see through. He feigned the regular breathing of someone in a deep sleep.

The door opened slowly, and he saw Bartocelli's silhouette against the light.

He'd come to check on him. The door closed.

Montalbano bolted out of bed and looked out of the porthole.

He couldn't see anything. The trawler must have pulled up along the other side.

He lay back down, listening for the slightest sound.

He realized Pennisi had come aboard when he heard the trawler's diesel engine moving away, and the *Halcyon*'s auxiliary engines start up again.

Knowing that Pennisi had arrived calmed him down a little.

It made the horror he'd seen mildly more tolerable. This enabled him to close his eyes and drift off to sleep.

SEVENTEEN

He hadn't noticed that the *Halcyon* had set all its sails during the night. Now, at the break of dawn, it was taking advantage of what bit of wind had risen and was skipping lightly across the sea like a capricious colt over a meadow of grass.

At ten minutes to seven Bartocelli came into the kitchen. He'd come to order them to divide the breakfast this time onto two large trays, one for the four crew members, and the second for the captain, himself, and the passenger who'd arrived during the night. The breakfast for the second group, however, was to be served in the salon. The chef and his assistant, as usual, were to remain in the kitchen. After Fazio left to set the tables, Bartocelli informed Montalbano that they were expecting six passengers to be coming onboard around noon, and that he should therefore prepare a luncheon in the salon for nine people. And he added that perhaps, though he wasn't entirely sure yet, the other passengers would be arriving around seven that evening. He would let Montalbano know in due course.

At this point Montalbano asked, somewhat provocatively: 'But do Verruso and I have to stay down here the whole time? I need to get some air.'

Bartocelli smiled.

'No problem at all! After breakfast, you can go up on deck and stay there until eleven.'

And he went out. Fazio returned, followed by a sailor who asked for the tray to take to the salon and then left. Fazio loaded up the tray for the crew and went out again.

When he returned, he sat down in front of the inspector to have some breakfast while Montalbano limited himself to drinking three coffees in a row. As Fazio ate he said he'd heard the sailors saying that there'd been a change of plan.

'In what sense?'

'I wasn't able to find out. But it seems the passengers who were expected to arrive two days from now will be coming in some time before midnight tonight. And apparently these passengers had to rent private aeroplanes and motorboats at the very last minute to get here ahead of schedule, though I never found out the reason.'

Montalbano remembered Pennisi saying that the participants were going to board the ship in a number of different Mediterranean ports. Apparently for some unknown reason they'd become anxious and needed to hurry things up. Maybe the discovery of Zaccaria's little betrayal had something to do with it? Who knew?

At any rate, so much the better. That meant fewer days to spend among these ferocious beasts.

Fazio then went to clear the tables and clean up in the mess hall and salon. He came back all excited.

'I got a glimpse of last night's passenger!'

'Pennisi?'

'I don't know what Pennisi looks like, Chief.'

'How'd it happen?'

'When I went to clear the table in the salon, there was nobody there. But on the table there was one of those inhaler cartridges, you know, the kind for asthma . . .'

'Yeah, go on.'

'Then suddenly a man came out from the little staircase leading from the cabins, but as soon as he saw me he turned around and went back.'

'Was he tall?'

'Yes.'

'Bald?'

Fazio hesitated. 'Bald? He had a head full of hair!'

Montalbano felt confused for a moment, then started laughing.

'What an idiot I am! He must have put on a wig to look like Contrera!'

He continued to feel reassured by Pennisi's presence.

'But,' Fazio said doubtfully, 'if he knew who I was, why didn't he stop and talk to me? He could at least have let me identify him.'

'What are you saying?' Montalbano fired back. 'How was he supposed to know that you were you after Santonastaso reduced you to such a state that your own mother, rest her soul, would never even recognize you?'

'Bah!' said Fazio, unconvinced.

'Listen, let's go up on deck and get some air. We have Bartocelli's permission.'

They sat down on the deck, astern, one beside the other, backs against a coil of cable.

As his lungs were blissfully filling with sea air, Montalbano closed his eyes and let the music carry him away.

The waves lapping against the bows, the water streaming against the ship's sides, the cracking of the sails, sharp as a rifle shot, the trilling of the rigging under stress, the shrill cawing of a seagull came together to form a sort of musical harmony.

After roughly half an hour of this, which had him nearly falling asleep, inside the music a different sound began to make itself heard, first softly, then more and more loudly, a continuous vibration.

He opened his eyes.

'What's that?' he asked Fazio.

'An aeroplane.'

At that moment Bartocelli came running out of the wheelhouse and towards them.

'I'm sorry, but you'll have to go back down below in fifteen minutes at the latest. The guests are arriving earlier than scheduled and don't want any strangers to see them. Discretion is rule number one on the *Halcyon*,' he concluded in the tone of a hotel manager.

The plane was flying low and slowly, at this point keeping even with the ship.

It was a little bigger than a Piper, grey, and bore the

inscription UR 342, written in white. One couldn't tell whether it was civilian or military. But when it flew over the schooner, Montalbano and the others noticed that it had a banner attached to the tailfin. It looked like one of those small aircraft that fly advertising streamers across the sky.

The banner featured four white squares divided by blue lines forming a cross.

Fazio bolted to his feet, pale as a ghost, watching the plane as though hypnotized. At that moment Bartocelli asked a sailor something a short distance away from them. When the sailor answered him, Bartocelli got angry and rushed back into the wheelhouse.

'What did he ask him?'

'He wanted to know what that banner meant, but for Christ's sake, even I know what it means: cease and desist, and it's intended for us. And the sailor explained to Bartocelli that that flag was an order to suspend everything and anything they were doing,' Fazio replied.

A sort of general commotion then broke out.

The captain emerged from the wheelhouse and gave two sharp, shrill whistles, and three sailors came up on deck as Bartocelli was yelling at Montalbano and Fazio: 'Go back down below!'

When they found themselves alone in the galley, Montalbano said: 'But what does all this mean?'

'Something must have gone wrong.'

'Then you know what I say? I'm going to go and ask Pennisi to explain.'

'You're insane!'

'It'll only take a few seconds.'

At that moment the schooner stopped. All the sails must have been taken in. But the auxiliary engines did not come on.

'I'm coming with you.'

'No, you stay here.'

And he left. In the twinkling of an eye, he was on the cabin deck.

All the doors were closed. Sweating, he started knocking lightly at every door. Nobody answered.

He was wasting precious time. Then he thought maybe Pennisi was in the salon.

He went back up the staircase and ever so slowly opened the door.

Pennisi was seated at the big table and reading something with his back to Montalbano.

Montalbano opened his half door all the way and began to enter. Pennisi sneezed.

The sneeze had the exact same effect on the inspector as a gunshot.

He froze and hunched over, tucking his head between his shoulders.

Pennisi, wanting to take out his handkerchief, turned partly to one side, and was now in profile. There was no boxer's nose, the lips were much thinner, and the shape of the face was not Pennisi's.

Frozen in terror, Montalbano still had the presence of mind to close the door without making the slightest sound. As he headed back to the kitchen, his legs were shaking.

*

'Calm down, Chief!' said Fazio, handing him a glass of water.

As he drank it the inspector heard the plane with the banner fly over again.

'I think the signal was given because Pennisi had been found out. And they may have killed him. Since, in fact, the person here in his place is Contrera himself.'

'There's one thing I don't understand, though,' said Fazio.

'What's that?'

'If they exposed Pennisi and liquidated him, how come you and I are still alive?'

'I think Pennisi worked in compartmentalized fashion, on a need-to-know basis. With each element discretely separate from the other. In my opinion, he was betrayed by someone on the trawler who must have been one of Contrera's men. But the men on the trawler knew nothing about Zaccaria. And vice-versa. At any rate, rest assured that when the cruise is over, they'll kill us, too. They don't want any witnesses whatsoever.'

'So what are we going to do?'

'We're forced to disobey the order to cease and desist. We have to neutralize these guys, or sooner or later they'll kill us.'

They heard the rumble of an approaching engine.

'I don't think that's the plane,' said Montalbano.

'No, it's a big motorboat.'

'So they're arriving. Now listen to me. The best thing is for us to start preparing lunch, and while I'm working on it I'll try to think of a way to get us out of this fix.'

'Can I say something, Chief?'

'Let's hear it.'

'Why don't we put the sedative in the food we're preparing now, and then call for help? Enough is enough. We settle for what we can get. The sooner we're out of this pickle the better.'

'That would be unfair to Pennisi,' the inspector said drily.

*

Ten minutes before the lunch was ready, two sailors came into the kitchen and wanted all the stuff for laying the table in the salon. Then, as soon as the *spaghetti alla Norma* was ready, Bartocelli and the same two sailors, as if they'd smelled the aroma, came in, loaded the trolley with the first-course dishes, and went out again.

'I should remind you that it's absolutely forbidden to enter the salon or go up on deck without my permission,' said Bartocelli. 'You've been well behaved so far, so keep up the good work. Oh, and I should also inform you that the remaining five guests will all be arriving together this evening around seven o'clock. That'll be the full contingent. So dinner at eight should be prepared for fourteen people. You two will continue to eat your meals in the kitchen.'

'I'm going to need to go to my cabin in the afternoon,' said Montalbano.

'Just let the sailor on guard know,' said Bartocelli.

'What about the crew's lunch?' asked Fazio.

'Two sailors will come and get it after they've served the guests.'

*

This time it was the sailors who saw to laying the table in the salon and cleaning up afterwards. Fazio was dismissed from even approaching the mess room.

It was clear that Bartocelli did not want to risk having him run into one of the bosses.

'Let's go into the pantry,' Montalbano said suddenly.

Overhead, on the main deck, they heard the captain's whistle ring out.

The sails were being set.

Fazio kept everything in perfect order. On the left, on the third shelf of a small cabinet, were all the spices: cloves, cinnamon, oregano, mint, thyme, and salt and pepper as well.

Montalbano opened the lone green packet of salt. He stuck the tip of his tongue in it, then spat.

'Sure tastes like salt to me,' he said, handing the bag to Fazio.

The other tasted it in turn. 'Yeah, it's salt.'

Cursing Catarella in his mind, the inspector opened the yellow bag of sugar and tasted it.

It had no flavour at all.

He handed it to Fazio, who also used the tip of his tongue.

'That's not sugar,' he said. Then, looking Montalbano in the eye, 'Is tonight the night?' he asked.

'Yes,' replied the inspector. 'Didn't Bartocelli say the full contingent will be here?'

They went out of the pantry.

'I'm going to go to my cabin for a bit,' said Montalbano.

'I'll stay here,' said Fazio.

As soon as he approached the staircase leading up to the deck, he saw the feet of a sailor.

'Hey!' he called to him.

The sailor turned around; he was armed with a submachine-gun. Montalbano, using gestures, let him know that he wanted to go to his cabin. The sailor signalled to him to come up and go to the other hatch. The *Halcyon* was cruising like a dream.

In front of the stern hatch, a second armed sailor, also gesturing, allowed him to go below, but followed him all the way to the door to his cabin. Montalbano went in and locked the door. It was possible the sailor remained outside standing guard.

But he himself had no intention of doing anything foolhardy.

By this point he'd made a decision. He only had to try to remain as calm as possible.

And so he lay down and closed his eyes.

*

At half-past four he got up, had a shower, left the cabin, and went up to the deck; the sailor on duty gave him the go-ahead, and he walked along the deck, breathing deep the fresh sea air, then went down into the galley.

Fazio was asleep in a chair, head thrown all the way back, mouth half open. Montalbano woke him up.

'We have to start getting dinner ready.'

'So soon?'

'Yeah, it's going to take a while.'

'Mind telling me what we're making?'

'Potato cake.'

'And for the second course?'

'I don't think they'll make it to the second course. But just to be safe, in case Bartocelli comes to check on us, we'll make some boiled chicken in green sauce.'

'What do we need from the pantry?'

'For the moment, get me a bag of potatoes. We can peel them together.'

When they'd finished peeling the potatoes, they sliced them and then put them in two big pans to cook. As soon as they were done, Montalbano drained them and then took a pestle and began to grind them until they became a kind of paste. He repeated the procedure with the potatoes from the second pan.

He then sent Fazio to get ten eggs, a bag of salt, and the yellow bag of sugar.

Five eggs per pan, salt and . . . How much sleeping powder?

Their very lives depended on the answer. Montalbano and Fazio looked at each other, questioning.

A pinch? A fistful?

Better to err on the side of excess.

The inspector put in two and a half handfuls for each pot, and as Fazio was taking the yellow sugar bag back to the galley, he began to knead the potato paste thoroughly with his hands.

Then he took two large baking dishes and spread one quarter of the potato mash in one. Fazio did the same with the other dish.

✲

They'd just finished when they realized that the *Halcyon* had stopped moving. A large engine could be heard approaching.

Montalbano looked at his watch. It was a quarter to seven.

So the rest of the guests were boarding the *Halcyon* a little early. Shouts, cries of greeting, and laughter were audible even in the galley.

They got back to work. Atop half the mashed potatoes they laid a filling of fontina cheese, grated Parmesan, a generous helping of ham, and olives. This they covered with the remaining potatoes. The inspector then had Fazio bring him a few more eggs and spread the whites over this top layer in both dishes.

'They need to bake for half an hour,' said Montalbano. 'We'll put them in the oven at seven twenty-five. For now we'll just let them sit.'

'And what are we going to eat?' asked Fazio.

'I think eating's the last thing we'll feel like doing.'

'But I'm hungry! I've got to eat, Chief!' Fazio protested.

The inspector gave him a funny look. 'What's got into you?'

'I guess it's not really hunger, Chief, but I'm nervous! It'll be the first time in my life I arrest eighteen people using a potato cake!'

'Look, there are four egg yolks here. Just whip up a couple with sugar, that'll calm you down.'

But he didn't calm down. As he was beating the eggs, he kept asking: 'Are you sure it's going to work, Chief?'

Or: 'Maybe we should've put in a little more?'

Or: 'Does it really take effect immediately?'

After a while Montalbano felt like bashing him in the head with a frying pan. But he controlled himself.

Because in fact he was asking himself the same questions as Fazio, just not aloud.

*

At a quarter to eight, two sailors came in to get the tableware. They returned at eight o'clock sharp with Bartocelli.

'Everything ready?'

'I think so,' said Montalbano, opening the oven.

A heavenly aroma filled the kitchen. The cake was perfectly cooked, the top layer of glaze having taken on a dark brown colour.

'Magnificent!' exclaimed Bartocelli. 'If it tastes as good as it smells . . .'

'Shall I cut it up?' asked Montalbano.

'No,' replied Bartocelli. 'Just cut four servings for the crew and put them on a separate tray. Then give us the dishes, that way everyone can take as much as he likes.'

The two sailors took one dish each while Bartocelli took the tray for the crew.

Left to themselves, Montalbano and Fazio silently hugged each other tight.

*

Then there was the problem of how to spend the next half-hour without succumbing to an attack of nerves or breaking out in tears.

'Your hands are shaking,' the inspector pointed out to Fazio.

'Why, aren't yours?' Fazio retorted.

And he started whistling passages from *Cavalleria Rusticana.*

For his part, Montalbano started reviewing in his head the opening lines of epic poems he'd studied in school: 'Sing, goddess, the anger of Peleus' son Achilleus/and its devastation . . .'

'Of ladies, cavaliers, of love and war . . .'

And every five minutes, they both looked at their watches.

Then they started circling about the kitchen, Montalbano clockwise, Fazio anticlockwise, and every so often they ran into each other but paid no mind.

By eight-forty, Montalbano couldn't take it any longer. 'I'm going to have a look,' he said.

He turned around and found the two sailors standing in front of him, having come to return the baking dishes and the empty tray. Fazio mechanically took them out of their hands. The two men just stood there, waiting.

They wanted the second course!

And he and Fazio had forgotten to make it!

More importantly, the sedative hadn't worked! And now, how the fuck . . .

Then, all at once, one of the two sailors' legs gave out, and he fell to the floor face-first. The other barely had the time to look bewildered before he leaned his back against the wall beside the door and slid slowly to the floor.

'It worked!' Montalbano shouted, so loudly that he made his own ears ring.

EIGHTEEN

'Let's take their guns!' was the first thing Fazio shouted as soon as he managed to recover from the tremendous scare he'd just had and could finally open his mouth. They raced up to the deck, crashing into each other and pushing as if there was a fire on board, but as soon as they were outside they saw no sailors on guard either awake or asleep.

The *Halcyon* advanced ever so slowly through the darkness of the night, its auxiliary engines at minimum throttle. Why hadn't they turned them off, now that everyone was aboard? Maybe the captain wanted to keep the ship continually in motion?

'I'm going to go down to the crew's mess,' said Fazio, heading for the fore hatch. 'That must be where the sailors are.'

Montalbano for his part went back down the poop-deck stairs and opened the door to the salon.

It was a shocking scene.

All fourteen men were sleeping. But they didn't look so much asleep as struck dead.

There were some with their heads thrown back, others with their faces plastered in their empty plates, others turned completely to one side, and one, who'd stood up halfway to grab a bottle of wine, sprawled out across the table.

Pennisi would have been rather pleased at the sight.

Montalbano dedicated it to him in his mind. But there was something that didn't add up. He counted the bodies. Thirteen.

One was missing.

And that one was Bartocelli.

Could he possibly have managed to . . . What was the explanation?

Surely he'd eaten the cake; he'd so loved the aroma when still in the kitchen . . .

But what now? Montalbano began to sweat. His heart raced, he felt out of breath.

Knowing that Bartocelli was lurking somewhere on the ship, which he didn't know very well, made his blood run cold.

Then he noticed that the door of one of the two salon toilets was half open. He approached and looked inside. And there was Bartocelli, out of action . . . Apparently he'd gone in there to relieve himself and was now on his knees, sleeping deeply with his head inside the toilet bowl.

But where was Fazio? Why hadn't he returned? The inspector raced over to the crew's mess.

There was only one sailor there, sitting at the table, sound asleep.

But no Fazio.

A sudden, irrational fear of having been left alone came over him. He felt like the lone survivor aboard a ghost ship.

He started running to the bows, opened the hatch, and called from the landing: 'Fazio!'

It came out sounding like the doleful howl of an abandoned dog.

'What's wrong, Chief?' came Fazio's voice, slightly shaken, from the crew's quarters.

Montalbano went down. But he was so agitated that he stumbled on the second step, and had he not been quick to grab the banister, he surely would have broken his neck.

Fazio was busy looking for the submachine-guns. Montalbano noticed that the fourth sailor wasn't here, either.

'A crewman is missing,' he said.

'Yeah, I noticed, Chief, and so I went looking for him. He's in the wheelhouse, fast asleep.' Then he suddenly burst out in rage: 'I can't find the fucking guns! Where the hell—'

'Never mind about that,' said the inspector. 'For the moment there's something more important to worry about than the submachine-guns.'

'And what would that be?'

'A roll of heavy cord.'

Fazio looked at him, not comprehending. 'What do we need that for?'

'Unless you have eighteen pairs of handcuffs on you . . .' Montalbano said, as if granting his point.

'You're right.'

'And we'd better move fast; we don't know how long the effect of the sedative will last.'

These words gave Fazio wings.

'You wait for me here,' he said. 'I know where to find some.'

He left and returned in a flash with a roll of thick cord and a sharp knife.

'Each man should be bound hand and foot,' said Montalbano. 'We need to cut eighteen pieces for their wrists, eighteen longer pieces for their ankles.'

They got down to work. Montalbano held the spool while Fazio cut.

'Other than tell you how the kitchen functioned, did the commissioner's office also tell you how to contact them so they could come and get us? Now's the time, while these guys are all asleep.'

'Yes, there are two available systems, and I know how to use both.'

When they'd finished cutting, Montalbano stuck the longer pieces of cord in his belt while Fazio did the same with the other pieces. They went back into the salon.

Nobody in the dormitory had moved, not even in their sleep. Fazio, who was seeing the scene for the first time, stopped dead in his tracks in shock.

'Come on, let's go,' said the inspector.

Division of labour: the sleepers' wrists were tied behind their backs by Fazio, their ankles by Montalbano, for whom it was a more tiring affair because he had to either move the chair the sleeper was sitting in or crouch down.

Once tied up, the man was then seized by the shoulders and feet and piled onto the others on the floor.

'I don't see Bartocelli!' Fazio suddenly exclaimed in alarm.

'Relax, he's sleeping in the toilet,' Montalbano reassured him.

When they got to Contrera, who was the last of the thirteen men at the table, Fazio didn't immediately tie his wrists up.

He studied him for a moment, then turned to the inspector, who had squatted to tie his ankles: 'Take a look at his face, Chief,' he said.

Montalbano stood up and looked at him. Contrera was greenish-grey.

'To me he looks dead,' said Fazio. 'Check his heart.'

Fazio put his head on the man's chest. 'He's dead,' he said after a pause.

'He suffered from asthma. Apparently . . .'

The inspector never managed to finish his sentence. Suddenly the *Halcyon* listed completely to starboard, emitting a sort of spine-chilling death groan.

The violent lurch caused Fazio to lose his balance, and he fell and rolled to the right in silence, unable to speak because of the shock and terror. Montalbano, likewise speechless and terrified, fell to the floor in turn, ending up smack against Fazio as a deluge of dishes, silverware, glasses, and bottles began to bury them.

Immediately the gloomy, monstrous siren of a gigantic steamship passing dangerously close to the *Halcyon* deafened them and left them stunned. Then the twelve inert bodies of the sleepers and the lifeless corpse, as if they'd spread the word among themselves, began to move in unison and, sliding across the tilting floor, re-formed their pile, further burying Fazio and Montalbano.

Seconds later, the schooner returned to its normal, upright position, and Fazio and Montalbano, with a tremendous effort of arms and legs, and the timely assistance of some powerful curses, managed to come out from under the mass of bodies and tableware.

'We miraculously averted a collision!' Fazio exclaimed, still out of breath.

Then he fell silent and his eyes opened wide.

The logical conclusion of the words he'd just uttered had terrified him.

If the *Halcyon* had veered at the last second, with such promptness and agility, that could only mean that there was someone at the helm. Someone awake. Quite awake.

It could only be the missing sailor.

The same one they'd seen asleep in the wheelhouse. Apparently he hadn't eaten much potato cake, and the sedative's effect hadn't lasted long at all.

Fazio turned around, eyes searching for Montalbano, whom he saw running for the door.

He must have come to the same conclusion.

Fazio shot to his feet and pulled up behind Montalbano.

'When you saw the sailor, are you sure he was armed?' Montalbano asked him.

'Absolutely certain.'

'Two against one, we'll manage.'

No sooner had they come out onto the deck through the stern hatch than they threw themselves facedown onto the floor, just to be safe.

They hadn't made the slightest sound. Hopefully the sailor hadn't noticed they'd come up on deck.

The *Halcyon*'s navigation lights made the darkness on the deck seem denser. In the wheelhouse there wasn't a single light on.

Ever so slowly, the inspector's eyes got used to the darkness, and things began to take on more precise contours.

On the floor, leaning against the left-hand side of the wheelhouse, was a motionless mass. Montalbano then managed to bring it into focus, but he wanted to be sure.

'When you saw the sailor, where was he?' he asked Fazio.

'Slumped over the helm, passed out.'

'Look over there,' said Montalbano.

Fazio must have had better vision. He replied almost at once.

'That's him.'

'But wasn't he lying on top of the helm?'

'I guess that when the ship lurched—'

'Rubbish! The lurch would have made him roll to the right, not the left! But, anyway, the point is that he could not have been at the helm steering the ship!'

'Who was it, then? A ghost? There's seventeen of them, plus the dead man.'

A thought flashed in Montalbano's brain. Their count was off.

They'd forgotten to tie up Bartocelli. 'You wait here. I'll be right back.'

Crawling along on his stomach, he made his way back to the stairs, went down to the salon, and ran to the bathroom.

As expected, it was empty.

Only then did he notice that the toilet bowl was full of vomit.

Bartocelli must have understood at once that there was something fishy in the cake and had run to throw up what he'd eaten. And, naturally, when Montalbano had come in, he'd pretended to be asleep. Then, when the inspector had gone to Fazio's quarters, the bastard had got up and gone into the wheelhouse.

But what had he been doing the whole time he was in there, while they were tying up the sleepers?

It was possible he'd got in touch with some other crooks of his ilk and called for help.

They urgently needed to flush him out.

Montalbano climbed the stairs to the last step, leaned out, grabbed one of Fazio's ankles, and pulled. Fazio got the message and, crawling along, joined him on the landing.

'Bartocelli's in the wheelhouse. We have to force him out.'

'Why? He shouldn't be armed by this point.'

'What makes you so sure?'

'Chief, if he had the submachine-guns, by now we'd be—'

'I don't trust that snake. And at any rate we have no choice but to take over the wheelhouse so we can radio our position to Mimì Augello. That was the plan.'

'But they told us to cease and desist!'

'But how can they be sure we saw the banner? They're just as uncertain as we are! Let's go!'

'Whatever you say.'

'You go up on deck through the stern hatch. I'll go up through this one. Before we do anything, I want to see if he's armed.'

As Fazio was walking away, the inspector went into the kitchen, took the big knife used for cutting meat, put two glasses into his pockets, and climbed the stairs.

The situation was the same as before.

He counted slowly to twenty to give Fazio time to get into position, then threw the first glass forcefully against the iron capstan holding the anchor chain.

A gunshot rang out from the wheelhouse. The bullet went *zing!* as it ricocheted off the capstan.

The son of a bitch could see in the dark, like a cat. He was armed with a revolver, not a submachine-gun, which was a point in his disfavour.

Montalbano was so engrossed in watching the wheelhouse that he didn't notice that Fazio had crawled up beside him.

'I told you . . .'

'Chief, we can't get him from behind. We have to make him come out.'

'How?'

'Theatrics, Chief.'

'OK.'

'Make some kind of noise. But close to us.'

The inspector tossed another glass out in a high arc in front of them.

The gunshot came immediately by way of reply. Just as immediately came Fazio's searing cry of pain. 'Aaahh! He got me!'

And continuing to wail and shout in desperation he dragged himself to the hatchway and lowered himself down.

Montalbano followed him, also shouting.

'Fazio! Where'd he hit you? Speak, for the love of God!'

'Aaaahhh!' was Fazio's reply.

They looked at each other and immediately understood. Montalbano shot off like a rocket, ran through the salon, opened the door, climbed the stairs, and popped out of the fore hatch.

And at once he saw the shadow of Bartocelli, who had his back to him and was cautiously approaching the stern hatch.

Even from there he could hear Fazio's howls.

The inspector bent down, removed his rope-soled shoes, and, reviving an animalesque nervous tension and agility he hadn't known since he was twenty years old, advanced through the darkness cautiously but swiftly, never once tripping over a cable or other obstacle, as if he knew the layout of the *Halcyon*'s deck by heart, and not even a searing pain in his left heel, certainly a shard of one of the glasses entering his flesh, could stop him.

Bartocelli, meanwhile, had reached the hatch and was now at its edge, bending forward, revolver extended in front of him.

Before going down the stairs, he wanted to know exactly where Fazio's increasingly feeble moans were coming from.

Standing less than a foot and a half behind him, Montalbano opened his mouth and filled his lungs with fresh sea air.

Then he called in a low voice: 'Bartocelli!'

The man shot up like a spring and turned around, but didn't have time to shoot.

The inspector's right hand had already sprung, and the razor-sharp blade of the meat knife sliced through fabric and flesh in an instant, penetrating deep into the intestines. At first Bartocelli leaned against Montalbano, then began to slide to the floor, bending forward over his knees, and this last movement enabled the blade, which was still in him, to tear him apart even more.

The inspector, shocked and paralysed, then summoned the strength to take a step backwards, freeing himself from Bartocelli's head and shoulders, which were still pressed against his legs.

Long shudders of disgust shook his body to the core, making him utterly unable to open his mouth to call Fazio.

In a moment of lucidity he saw that he was holding Bartocelli's revolver in his left hand.

He'd disarmed him while knifing him and hadn't realized it.

At that moment the *Halcyon* became brightly lit, as if it was suddenly daylight. The powerful illumination, which was coming from the sea, blinded Montalbano and forced him to cover his eyes with his forearm.

Moments later he heard the heavy steps of a few men running across the deck.

He was certain they were the reinforcements Bartocelli had summoned.

And if that was the case, it had all been for naught. He heard a voice barely three feet away order him: 'Drop the gun and put your hands up!'

He did nothing of what he'd been ordered. Instead he lowered his arm and opened his eyes.

Before him stood Mimì Augello.

And he was holding a revolver in both hands and pointing it at him, arms extended and legs spread and flexed. The regulation stance for shooting. Had Augello completely lost his mind?

'Mi . . .' the inspector began with effort, as the emotion inside him was throttling his breathing and heart. He was trying to say, 'Mimì.'

Augello repeated his command.

'Drop your weapon and put your hands up!'

What the hell was he doing? Was this some kind of joke? At a moment like this? It was really uncalled for!

'Mi . . .' Montalbano tried again.

Mimì's kick got him square in the belly, knocking the

wind out of him and doubling him over, and the blow from the butt of Mimì's revolver to the back of his head did the rest.

A split-second before losing consciousness, Montalbano realized that, thanks to Santonastaso, Mimì Augello hadn't recognized him.

And consoled by this awareness – if you could really call it a consolation – he relinquished consciousness.

*

He awoke in a hospital bed, the back of his head aching and bandaged. He knew he was Inspector Salvo Montalbano, but he had no recollection of how or why he'd ended up in that room. With some effort, he managed to turn his head a little.

Sitting up in the other bed was a man with very curly white hair and a bandaged chest.

'Welcome back,' the man said.

'Thank you. Can you tell me where we are?'

'In a hospital in Malta.'

How had he ended up in Malta?

The other man intuited his question.

'It was the nearest place.'

Nearest to what?

'And why did they—'

'Concussion.'

'I see. And why are you here, if you don't mind my asking?'

'Gunshot wound. From the same person who struck

you. Inspector Augello. But he didn't do it on purpose; he just didn't recognize us. Do you really not remember me, Chief? I'm Fazio!'

The inspector gave a start. Of course he remembered Fazio, but . . .

'But you don't look like him.'

'You don't look like yourself, either. There's a mirror on your left. Think you can manage to look at yourself?'

He could manage. That hair colour, the cut of the moustache . . . It wasn't him.

He turned back towards Fazio. 'Tell me what happened.'

As Fazio was speaking, Montalbano's memory began to return, but dimly, as if seen by the glow of a night-light. When Fazio came to the fact that Pennisi had never boarded the ship, he interrupted him.

'Has anyone found out what happened?'

'Yeah, you were right. They recognized him and slit his throat.'

'Go on.'

Fazio explained how, once they found out Pennisi had been killed, the FBI had decided to scuttle the plan. They were going to attack the *Halcyon* instead. Which in fact they did, not knowing, however, that they would find everyone asleep.

And at that moment the glow of the night-light in Montalbano's head turned into the blinding glare of the floodlights illuminating the deck of the *Halcyon* like the noonday sun.

And he saw himself again behind Bartocelli, felt again

in his right hand the blunt force of the knife cutting through flesh, the sensation travelling from the hand squeezing its handle on up to his brain and then down to his mouth in a suppressed cry of horror that raged through his body like a violent wind.

'No!' he shouted.

'Are you tired?'

'Yes.'

He closed his eyes. He had made a decision.

He would arrange things so that this story would never be his. He would disown it, erase it forever from his memory.

Aboard the *Halcyon* there had been a man with a different name and a different face.

A complete unknown.

Author's Note

This story was conceived about ten years ago, not as a novel but as a script for an Italian and American film co-production. When the plans for collaboration fell through, I used the screenplay, with a few variants, for a new Montalbano book, and I suppose that, for better or for worse, the non-literary origins of the work show through in the telling.

As usual I declare that this latest novel, too, is entirely the fruit of my imagination.

Notes

6 ***Eau si claire et si pure*:** From 'La chanson de l'eau', a traditional French song.

18 ***pasta alla carrittera*:** A simple pasta dish with a spicy tomato sauce containing a great deal of garlic, hot pepper, and parsley.

36 raised his arm halfway as they did at Pontida: Pontida is the town in northern Italy where the far-right party, La Lega, periodically holds its summits.

40 If the man assumed a threatening air he would headbutt him à la Zidane: This is a reference to the infamous *coup de boule* that French star midfielder Zinédine Zidane gave to Italian defender Marco Materazzi in the closing minutes of regulation time of the 2006 World Cup soccer final, upon verbal provocation from the Italian defender. The headbutt led to Zidane's expulsion from the game, depriving France of their best striker, which may have cost them dearly in the shootout by which the outcome was finally determined after regulation play ended in a draw. Italy won the shootout 5–3.

43 a lance corporal leaning against the carabinieri squad car: The carabinieri are a nationalized police force and a branch of the army, and their ranks are military in character.

45 for the CFRB: Comando Forze Repressione Banditismo, a long-defunct sector of the national carabinieri designated, just after the end of the Second World War, to combat banditry in Sicily and the deep south of Italy.

72 'Trincanato reported the incident to the carabinieri': The carabinieri and local police forces are separate bureaucracies and often in competition with one another. (See note to page 43.)

89 'everything around here is called Cristoforo Colombo': Christopher Columbus, though he sailed for the Queen and King of Spain, was originally from Genoa, and the city is full of reminders of this.

120 He must, therefore, have involved other authorities, the prefect, at the very least: In the Italian bureaucracy, the prefect is the local representative of the central national government.

129 *The Great Cemeteries Under the Moon* was the title of a book by a French author he'd read many years before: This is *Les Grands cimetières sous la lune*, 1938, by Georges

Bernanos, known in English under the title *A Diary of My Times*.

145 I advise you to call the carabinieri, not the police: See note to page 43.

152 Do you think you can just come here and play if you catch a Turk, he's yours?: A Sicilian expression used to gently rib someone who takes undue advantage of a situation, such as, say, pinching pennies or making oneself too presumptively at home in someone else's house, as Pennisi metaphorically does here.

185 *'In bocc'al lupo!' . . . 'Crepi'*: The Italian way of wishing someone good luck without jinxing them (like 'break a leg' in English). It means 'Into the jaws of the wolf,' and the recipient of the wish must reply '*Crepi*' ('May the wolf die') for the superstition to be most effective.

189 *'Farewell, lighthouse rising from the waters and into the sky'*: A slightly modified quotation from the nineteenth-century classic novel by Alessandro Manzoni, *The Betrothed* (*I promessi sposi*), chapter VIII. The original actually says, 'Farewell, mountains rising from the waters and into the sky' (*Addio, monti sorgenti dall'acque, ed elevati al cielo*).

204 *spaghetti alla chitarra . . . spaghetti all'aglio e olio*: *Spaghetti alla chitarra* is an egg-based pasta originally from the Abbruzzi-Puglia region that looks like cruciform spaghetti. *Spaghetti all'aglio e olio* is the simplest way to prepare spaghetti, with a sauce of olive oil in which several cloves of garlic have been sautéed, and, optionally, some hot pepper.

235 *spaghetti alla Norma*: *Alla Norma* sauces for pasta consist principally of tomato and aubergine.

241 'Sing, goddess, the anger of Peleus' son Achilleus' . . . 'Of ladies, cavaliers, of love and war': The quotes are, respectively, the opening lines of Homer's *Iliad* (translated by Richmond Lattimore, University of Chicago Press, 1951) and of *Orlando Furioso*, by Ludovico Ariosto (translated by Barbara Reynolds, Penguin Books, 1975).

Notes by Stephen Sartarelli